Her body thrilled at the sight of this man in her living room.

It had been just her and Alexa for so long. Not that their tiny family wasn't enough. She had everything she needed for a lifetime of happiness—a safe, dry home, a few good friends and a bright, healthy daughter. She had never felt any lack in her new life in Twin Creeks.

And yet...Joe's masculine energy was stirring something in her that she thought had died long ago. It was like realizing that cake was pretty good, but cake with icing, well, that was a decadent treat. She wasn't sure if this was good or not. On the one hand, it meant she was still alive. A healthy, vibrant woman with robust sexual appetites. But it felt dangerous, too. Like opening a Pandora's box of forbidden desires that could trample her fragile life if she surrendered. She swallowed hard, straightened her sweater and joined him in the living room...

Dear Reader,

Joe believes being a great doctor means working harder than anyone else. But his mentor won't support his fellowship until he learns to treat patients, not just diseases. Whatever that means!

Now this big-city, no-strings-attached playboy doc is stuck in Nowhere, Montana. Population: 2,000. Weather: dreadful. Things get worse when a snowmobile crash wrecks his shoulder and traps his beloved dog, Daisy. Luckily, he's within hiking distance of a cozy cabin...

Lily used to save critically injured patients as a flight trauma nurse, but after her husband's tragic death, Twin Creeks became her refuge—a quirky, close-knit community where she could raise her daughter in peace. Until a blizzard drops a handsome stranger on her doorstep. Now she can't deny that a life without risk is a life without joy.

If you love a good fish-out-of-water story, this one's for you! I adore watching overconfident characters stumble in unfamiliar territory. While I had fun at Joe's expense, I gave him Lily, a wounded single mom who inspires Joe to open his heart and offer her all the love and healing she deserves.

Let's hang out! Find me at katemacguire.com or on social media (@katewritesromance)!

Kate MacGuire

CITY DOC FOR THE
SINGLE MOM

KATE MacGUIRE

MEDICAL ROMANCE

Harlequin®
MEDICAL
ROMANCE

Recycling programs for this product may not exist in your area.

ISBN-13: 978-1-335-94303-3

City Doc for the Single Mom

Harlequin Enterprises ULC
22 Adelaide St. West, 41st Floor
Toronto, Ontario M5H 4E3, Canada
www.Harlequin.com

Printed in U.S.A.

Kate MacGuire has loved writing since forever, which led to a career in journalism and public relations. Her short fiction won the Swarthout Award and placed third in the 2020 Women's National Book Association writing contest. Medical romance has always been her guilty pleasure, so she is thrilled to be writing novels for Harlequin's Medical Romance line. When she's not pounding away on the keyboard, Kate co-runs Camp Runamuk with her husband, keeping its two unruly campers in line in the beautiful woodlands of North Carolina. Visit katemacguire.com for updates and stories.

Books by Kate MacGuire

Harlequin Medical Romance

Resisting the Off-Limits Pediatrician

Visit the Author Profile page at Harlequin.com.

For Nate and Megan: every day you inspire me
to tell—and live—the stories that matter.

CHAPTER ONE

"WINTER STORM ISABELLA'S cross-country trek is underway, but the worst of its impacts are still to come as it spreads heavy snow and blizzard conditions through the Rockies, Plains and upper Midwest. Folks, the National Weather Service is calling this storm historic *for our area, so please avoid all unnecessary travel and be prepared to hunker down for a few days."*

Lily switched off the radio as she glided to a stop alongside the Shop-n-Go, the small, locally owned grocery store on Twin Creeks's Main Street. Stocked with everything from milk and butter to deer corn and cast-iron cookware, the Shop-n-Go was pretty much the hub of activity in the final hours before any big storm. So it was no surprise to Lily that all the parking spots in front of the store were taken.

But luckily for her, a brown sedan was backing out of its space. She flicked her turn signal on to let the cars behind her know she was waiting for that spot. The sedan driver gave her a little wave before motoring off, the car's exhaust pipe emitting white smoke on this bitterly cold day.

Lily smiled and waved back, not sure if she knew the driver. She had met her fair share of neighbors and friends since she had moved to the former mining community of Twin Creeks five years earlier with her newborn daughter, Alexa. But it didn't matter. Even if they were strangers, the driver would have waved. That was just how it was in Twin Creeks, especially during the off-season when the tourists were gone and the town returned to a slower, more civilized, pace.

Lily eased her foot off the brake. Her truck made a creaky, wheezy sound as it slowly coasted forward. She loved this old truck, as much as she had loved the cherry-red convertible sportster that had been her ride when she lived in Chicago. But that little cutie was no match for the unpaved road riddled with divots that wound through thick forests to her tiny cabin. The old, sturdy flatbed truck that once hauled produce for a hydroponic farm had no trouble grinding its way up the hills to the cabin Lily rented from Jennifer Wilkins, a widow who lived in the main house. One of these days she'd get around to removing The Lettuce Lab's company decals from the truck's doors.

Lily was about to pull in to her spot when a streak of black whipped past her and claimed her parking space. Music—loud and thumping—pulsed from the car's interior. The streak turned out to be a midnight-black expensive luxury car, its sleek, aerodynamic lines and shiny, rust-free paint hinting at faraway places. Her hunch was confirmed by the car's blue-and-white license plate that said the car was registered in the coastal state of California.

The music stopped. The car door opened, and a man unfolded himself from the driver's seat. He was tall and dressed in khakis, a light blue dress shirt and a rust-toned hooded sheepskin jacket, which was paired with a casually tousled haircut that would have cost two hundred dollars or more in Chicago. Lily couldn't help but stare at a man who looked like he had just stepped out of the catalog for a high-end outdoor retailer. Even without the California license plate, his whole vibe screamed *I'm not from around here!*

There was no apologetic wave to acknowledge he had just stolen her parking spot. Instead, the man opened his back door. A lean black-and-white dog jumped out, then sat attentively at his side. The man turned on his heel, pointing his key fob over his shoulder to activate the car's alarm system with a sharp *beep-beep*. He strode into the Shop-n-Go on long legs, his hands tucked deep into his jacket with the dog trotting obediently at his side.

"What the...?" Lily began, then forced her slack jaw to shut. She, like most locals, was used to summer visitors traipsing all over their town with little regard for basic manners as they explored the endless miles of hiking trails and top-notch breweries. But the winter months were for the locals, along with a few *respectful* tourists who craved Twin Creeks's quieter winter ski season.

Her gaze fell to the car's bumper where a decal declared the car's owner liked to *Work Hard. Play Harder!* So there it was. Just another winter visitor who was more focused on making the most of his ski weekend than practicing a little common decency.

But boy, had he picked the wrong weekend for a ski trip. Lily was no stranger to the mountains of snow that Montana winters could deliver. But even she was a little nervous about this *epic storm*. In a state accustomed to measuring snow in feet rather than inches, calling a winter storm *historic* was not a good omen.

Lily found a parking spot behind the Shop-n-Go. She slammed the truck's heavy door shut and headed inside, a cloth bag slung over her shoulder. Glass jars clinked against each other with every step. By the time she arrived, she had forgotten all about the rude tourist and was back to humming along with a tune that had been playing in her head all morning. She couldn't remember the lyrics, but it didn't matter. The tune itself was upbeat and positive, like something good was about to happen.

Before entering the store, Lily looked to the sky, where gray clouds were clumping into thicker, darker ones by the hour. Oh, yes, good things were definitely about to happen.

Because Winter Storm Isabella meant at least two days alone with her little girl. With any luck, the power would go out sooner rather than later, giving Lily a legitimate excuse to ignore her work for a few days. Being the clinical editor for a nursing journal sure lacked the thrill of her former job as a trauma flight nurse practitioner, but it paid the bills and kept her and Alexa safe, so she couldn't complain too much.

But first, a little unofficial business. Edith

was running the cash register as always. Lily paused her whistling long enough to call out a greeting. As soon as she saw Lily's cloth bag, Edith rolled her eyes.

"Sweet Mary, not more pickles," she groaned. "I still haven't sold the last dozen you gave me!"

"This is the last batch!" Lily said with a laugh. Which wasn't entirely true. All the energy she used to funnel into her work as a flight nurse was now directed to her new hobby farm. The result had been quite the bumper crop of cucumbers over the summer. There were at least a dozen more jars lined up in Lily's pantry that needed a home. But Edith didn't need to know that just yet.

Edith shoved the bag under the counter and gave Lily a look that let her know that she better not see any more pickles for a good long while. Lily scooted to the back of the store before Edith could scold her again.

The refrigerated cases were predictably empty. Lily didn't have much time to shop. She didn't want Alexa to be the last one to be picked up from her home-based preschool. That would do nothing to get their little winter retreat off to a good start.

Lily quickly scanned the shelves, looking for games or crafts that Alexa might like. A picture frame tucked behind the painting kits and modeling clay caught her eye. She grabbed the frame and studied its photo of a fake family. A dad, a mom and a little girl eating ice cream at some kind of carnival. Geez, they looked stupid happy. Did Alexa ever feel as happy as that little girl looked? Lily wasn't sure.

Alexa wasn't a tiny toddler anymore, content with playground adventures and library story times. She was becoming more adventurous and bold—the same traits that had once motivated Lily to become a trauma nurse in the army and then a flight nurse practitioner for an air ambulance company in Chicago.

But Alexa had never known that version of Lily. Because those traits died the same day her husband did. Now all she cared about was keeping Alexa safe, no matter what. That meant saying no to Alexa's growing wish list of Grand Life Adventures.

Could I please ski something harder than the bunny slope?

Too much risk of head trauma, even with a helmet.

When can I go to a sleepover party?

The thought of Alexa being away overnight made Lily hyperventilate.

And Alexa's final, brazen request: *I want to go to kindergarten next year.*

Kindergarten. Whoever thought Lily would fear kindergarten? But Connor's death had changed everything. That was the day she'd learned gunmen could show up anywhere—even a hospital's emergency room—and steal the person you loved most for absolutely no good reason.

And if that utterly random act of violence left her a widow, what could happen to Alexa?

I don't know, Alexa. We'll see.

That was the best she could manage when Alexa would bring the topic up again and again. But the unresolved conflict had left its mark on their relationship.

So Lily couldn't wait for Isabella to arrive. It meant two days alone with her precocious daughter, surrounded by books and games and hot chocolate and cozy quilts. With any luck, she and Alexa would be able to regain the closeness they'd once shared.

Lily sighed and put the happy family back on the store shelf. She knew nothing in that photo was real, but she couldn't deny how much she wanted her and Alexa to feel *that* happy, just for one single day.

   That was when she felt something cold and wet tickle the back of her neck.

Lily shrieked in shock and surprise and instinctively jumped away from the unfamiliar sensation. She landed awkwardly on her butt in a most undignified fashion.

   Her abuser gave her a slow, thoughtful blink, then sat on its haunches and considered her with a cocked head and liquid brown eyes.

   "What," Lily sputtered, "the hell?"

   The dog stretched forward to press its muzzle into her hand. Its touch was gentle and seemed intentional. Not dangerous, at least not so far.

   She reached down to stroke its silky head, finding a blue collar with black stripes and sparkly rhinestone diamonds.

   "Daisy," she read. "Is that you?" The dog, some kind of mix of Border collie and who knew what else, wagged her tail slowly, enjoying Lily's gentle ear rub.

   A man's voice rang out. "Daisy! You little minx. Where are you?"

   Daisy cocked her head in the direction of the man's voice. Then she turned back to Lily with an open-mouthed pant. If Lily didn't know better, she'd swear the dog was laughing.

"We better get you reunited with your owner," Lily said. Then she added, under her breath, "And hey, do me a favor, would you? Tell him not to steal parking spots. It's rude."

"Who stole your parking spot?"

Lily winced at realizing she had been overheard. She stood and turned to find Mr. Work Hard Play Harder appraising her with captivating blue eyes.

By all appearances, the traveler was living up to his vehicular motto. His clothes were high-end but seemed casually tousled in a way that was probably anything but casual. He wore his dark brown wavy hair swept away from his face, revealing smooth skin, piercing blue eyes and a light stubble beard that had been precisely trimmed to perfection.

Lily's first thought was that he must be a tech bro. One of those guys who had created a social media app for teenagers and made a fortune larger than the GDP of most third-world countries. But he wasn't sporting the requisite tech bro hoodie or backpack, so maybe not. Stockbroker? Could be. He lacked that California-sunshine-and-avocado-toast vibe, so it was possible he spent his day in front of multiple monitors, tracking stocks and commodities. Lawyer or accounting executive worked, too.

Whatever he did for a living, he must be doing it well enough to afford the good life. But that didn't give him the right to be rude.

"Well, to be honest, you did."

His eyebrows, thick and precisely trimmed, arched as he quickly scanned her from head to toe. Her mouth went dry as she remembered the heavy-duty, super-functional overalls she was wearing. And the even more functional— and ugly—rubber boots she had donned before dawn to deal with the snow-and-mud slushy mix that was the current state of her farm.

She just hoped she didn't have any chicken feathers stuck to her hair. Or her butt.

He didn't seem particularly offended at her accusation. If anything, he appeared amused. He tucked his shopping basket over one arm and leaned against the shelving where jars of pickles and olives were lined up in neat rows.

His smile was disarming, as was his husky voice. "Sure it was me?" Mischief sparkled in his eyes like they were at a bar— instead of a small-town grocery store—and he wanted to buy her a drink.

She mentally replayed her first sighting of him. The sharp angles of his jaw and his confident stride as he walked into the Shop-n-Go. She swallowed hard, now aware that she had unabashedly checked him out in the parking lot. So yes, she was sure it was him.

"I remember your dog," was the best explanation she could conjure.

His brow furrowed as he seemed to search his memory bank. "Oh, wait! Were you in that old, beat-up pickup truck?" The words must have popped out before he could consider his tone. He grimaced. "Sorry. That came out wrong."

She waved off his apology. "Yeah, that was me."

"I had no idea you were waiting. I thought you were there to deliver produce or something."

So he thought she was a lettuce farmer, for which, considering her overalls and her ride, she could hardly blame him. It shouldn't matter what he thought—he was just a tourist. Still, his attention made her feel overly self-conscious.

"I don't know how things work where you come from Mr....?"

"Chambers." He stepped forward with an utterly disarming smile and offered his hand. "Joe Chambers."

His hand, warm and strong, clasped hers for just a moment, the simple touch igniting a spark that lingered long after his fingers slipped away. She looked up to find his gaze studying her, which only intensified the warmth that seemed to diffuse from his hand into her body.

She cleared her throat and massaged her tingling hand. She would have liked a moment to catch her breath, but Mr. California was waiting for a response while she was finding words hard to come by.

She cleared her throat. "Mr. Chambers, here in Twin Creeks, we use turn signals to show we're waiting for a parking spot. Perhaps you missed mine on account of how fast you were going?"

Good grief, she sounded just like her fourth-grade teacher. Formal to the point of brittle.

Joe chortled. "I doubt it. How fast could I go in Nowhere, Montana, with a giant produce truck blocking my lane?"

Nowhere, Montana? What the...?

He held up his hand in a defensive gesture. "I'm sorry. That was rude." His gaze drifted downward to his lace-up leather boots. His smile slipped and she saw fatigue in the crinkles around his eyes, a slight slump to his shoulders. He looked up to meet her gaze, his blue eyes intense and sincere. "It's just…been a day."

His comment *was* rude. But her irritation refused to stick. Those prominent cheekbones and deep blue eyes were making it hard to stay focused on a stupid parking spot.

"Well, okay then," Lily replied, her words having decided to take an impromptu vacation. "Just, you know, look where you're going next time." She mentally face-palmed herself for her schoolmarmish scolding. Why didn't she just waggle her finger at him for good measure?

Joe smiled as his gaze lingered on her lips. She saw some kind of shift in his expression that she couldn't quite read. Less fight, more… *what*? Interest? That didn't make sense. She had literally come straight from farm chores to the Shop-n-Go without a smidge of lipstick or a decent outfit.

"Thank you, ma'am. I will be sure to do that." He gifted her one last wistful smile before he turned on his heel and whistled. Daisy whimpered softly, then fell in step with her person, her hips swaying in rhythm with her foot strikes.

Lily watched them leave, her hands still

fisted on her hips. She felt disoriented and faintly flustered. What had just happened? Did she win? She wasn't sure. If so, winning had left her with a hollow, unsettled feeling.

Just then, her cell phone alarm beeped, warning her of Alexa's impending school dismissal. She chose the rock-painting kit, tossed it into her basket and headed for the checkout.

Lily took her spot behind Grace Brown, the town's sole art gallery owner, in the checkout line. Lily checked the weather radar on her phone. Blizzard conditions would start after nightfall. She had plenty of time to get Alexa from preschool, then spend the afternoon baking and watching movies.

Lily had just started scrolling through cookie recipes when Grace suddenly dropped to her knees. Her shopping basket slipped from her hands, sending batteries skittering across the floor.

Then she fell forward, unconscious.

Edith screamed and pressed her hands to her mouth. "Oh, my God, she's having a heart attack!"

Maybe. But it could be a stroke. Or low blood sugar? Lily knelt down and gently rolled Grace to her back. She hadn't used her nursing training for over five years, but she remembered everything she'd been taught.

Lily placed a hand on Grace's forehead and gently tilted her head back, making sure her airway was open. Then she placed her ear over Grace's mouth, hoping to feel Grace's warm breath on her cheek or hear sounds of her breathing.

Nothing.

Lily reflexively reached for the stethoscope she used to drape around her neck. But of course, it wasn't there. So she placed two fingers on the side of Grace's neck, desperately hoping she'd find a steady pulse. But there was no flutter beneath her fingers. Not in her neck nor in her wrists.

Grace was in cardiac arrest. For reasons Lily couldn't know without testing, her heart had stopped beating. There was a small chance she would survive, but only if she received intensive medical care very soon.

Lily knew exactly what she needed to do—tear Grace's coat aside and yank up her shirt, then brace the palms of her hands against Grace's sternum and deliver a staccato of hard chest compressions.

But Lily's hands remained fisted at her sides.

Oh, no, not now. Not with Grace.

Her body was a stubborn, useless statue. She desperately wanted to leap into action to save Grace's life. Her brain even screamed *Move!* so loud, Lily flinched.

But she remained frozen in place, her tight chest sucking in tiny gulps of air.

She's going to die, Lily, right in front of you, if you don't do something.

Just like Connor had died. His body sprawled on the floor of the emergency room where he saved patients every day, but where his trauma team could not save him. Not even with Lily crouched at his side, futilely trying to contain the red flower that bloomed across his chest.

We're losing him! Get the crash cart now!

Frantic voices crossed five years of memories to slam her right back into the worst day of her life. She wiped her sweaty palms on her overalls. She didn't want to be here. Didn't want to experience these muscle memories that made it feel like that night was happening all over again.

The door was so close. All she had to do was drop her basket and run. Maybe if she could get outside, this fog would lift and she would be able to think again. To breathe.

But no, she couldn't do that. Not with Grace

in her arms, slipping away. She squeezed her eyes shut against the horror unfolding before her.

Because she knew she couldn't save Grace. Her body wouldn't let her.

She never knew when these panic attacks would flare. They had started a few months after Connor died, when she'd tried to return to work. She'd thought it was a fluke at first—just a bad day, fatigue, whatever, but she was wrong. The more urgent or traumatic the call-out was, the more likely she was to stand frozen on the sidelines, hands fisted at her sides, watching helplessly as her trauma team did all the hard work without her.

Her coworkers had been kind, and her boss was understanding. There was talk of more time off, support groups, counseling. But Lily knew the rules. There was no room on a medevac helicopter for someone who couldn't pull her weight.

That was why she had left everything she loved in Chicago. Her job, the fast pace of city life, her friends and neighborhood.

All so she could keep Alexa safe from the unpredictable side of city life. And make sure that her flaws never, ever hurt a sick or injured patient.

But her past had caught up to her here in Twin Creeks. She bowed her head in despair, barely aware of Edith's frantic cries for someone to please, for Pete's sake, help Grace!

But then a streak of rust-toned coat and dark hair appeared in her peripheral vision. Before she could register what was happening, the dark-haired stranger who stole her parking spot slid to Grace's side on his knees.

"What happened?"

"She's having a heart attack!" Edith screamed. "We need a doctor!"

"I *am* a doctor," Joe replied. He lifted Grace's eyelids, using his cell phone's flashlight to check her reflexes. He seemed utterly calm and focused, as if he had come to the Shop-n-Go for the sole purpose of saving Grace's life.

After checking Grace's pulse, Joe whipped off his jacket, rolled up his sleeves, and pressed the palms of his hands against her chest.

His quick action and laser focus was enough to shock Lily out of her panic attack. Daisy had followed Joe and seemed to know this was serious. She dropped to the floor and appraised Lily with her serious brown eyes.

Lily's vise grip around her chest loosened just a bit. It felt good not to be alone anymore.

Joe's steady pace and single-minded focus on Grace gave her something to concentrate on. She started silently counting each of Joe's compressions, then pinched Grace's nose shut and delivered a full breath while Joe waited. Soon, they were working in harmony, his chest compressions to her breaths. Her anxiety slowly receded, allowing her mind to clear so she remembered something important.

"Edith! Call the high school! Ask them to bring the defibrillator over—stat!"

Joe's gaze caught hers. "Shouldn't emergency services be here by now?"

"We share emergency services with six other rural towns in western Montana. They could be here in five minutes…or an hour."

Joe was utterly focused on his work. His arms were straight and rigid, his entire body working to deliver the deep, hard chest compressions that Grace needed to keep her heart and brain oxygenated. Sweat beaded on his forehead and upper lip. Maybe he was a jerk when it came to parking spaces, but Lily felt profoundly grateful their paths had crossed that day.

"I can take over. You've been working for two minutes," she said. "You run lead on the defibrillation when the AED gets here."

Joe glanced up, his eyes searching hers, filled with unspoken questions.

"I used to be a flight nurse," she explained. Lily waited until his twenty-count was done before lacing her hands together and taking Joe's place. "But that was a long time ago," she added, her tone somber as she began her count to twenty.

CHAPTER TWO

THE SOUND WAS very far away—muffled and indistinct, like it was coming from a deep tunnel. And so annoying, like a persistent bee.

It was a bell, ringing over and over and over.

Joe groaned and reached for his phone. His thick *Practical Medical Oncology* textbook slipped from his lap and landed on the floor with a thud, startling Daisy from her nap.

A booming male voice started talking before Joe could even say hello. "Bill needs his insulin."

"I'm sorry...what?"

"Bill Parker."

Joe recognized the caller as George Benson, the mayor of Twin Creeks. George had led Joe's video interview with the town council to be Twin Creeks's interim doctor until they found a permanent replacement. The previous doctor had run the town's sole medical clinic for four decades before succumbing to heart disease. Despite months of running job postings around the country, the council had not found anyone willing to relocate to the former mining community nestled at the foot of a mountain.

"Lives over in Blue Sky Valley. He's out of insulin and he's going to need it before he gets shut in by the blizzard."

Joe unfolded his bone-weary body from the recliner where he had fallen asleep watching a hockey game. He tossed his blanket back on the chair and rolled his shoulders and neck, feeling a deep ache from the grueling marathon session of saving Grace's life at the Shop-and-Go.

It had taken the EMT team forty-five minutes to arrive. By then, he and Lily had performed CPR nonstop, pausing only to deliver shocks with the portable AED machine. He'd never been so happy to hear the sound of sirens in his life. Even happier to learn that the EMT could detect Grace's persistent, if tachy, pulse.

Joe opened his front door to look at the storm. Snow fell sideways, driven by a steady, brisk wind. The cold air sliced through his T-shirt and stung his eyes.

"You want me to drive to Bill Parker's house in this weather?" Tiny shards of ice pelted his face, driving him back into his warm, dry house.

"Well, he's out of insulin, isn't he?" The mayor's tone was matter-of-fact, as if driving through blizzards was a normal occurrence around here.

"Couldn't the pharmacy courier the insulin to him?"

"Courier? What?"

Of course not. Joe was acting like he was still a resident doctor back in Los Angeles, working in a top-tier hospital with armies of medical specialists at his beck and call. Back there, he could have phoned in a script from the comfort of his recliner. The pharmacy would have filled the prescription and delivered it by private courier, charging it all to the patient's insurance.

But those days were long behind him now. His residency was over and his plans to train for a career in oncology had ended in a spectacular plot twist he had never seen coming. Instead of being halfway through the first year of a top oncology fellowship, he had been exiled to Nowhere, Montana, and now had to figure out what on earth the mayor wanted from him.

"Never mind. Could this wait until the storm passes?"

"No can do, Doc. Bill's caretaker saw my wife at the feed-and-tack store this morning. She said that Bill dropped his last vial of insulin when he did his injection this morning. So now he's out and needs more."

"And I'm just hearing about this now?" Joe ran a hand through his hair. Good grief, what if the council member's wife hadn't gone to the feed-and-tack store? Would Bill just muddle through without his insulin, risking his body going into diabetic ketoacidosis?

Joe could practically hear the man shrug. "First I thought of it, I guess."

Joe opened the front door again, squinting his eyes against the wind and ice. He could barely see a foot beyond his front door. "I'm sorry, but these roads simply aren't drivable."

Not in his luxury sedan anyway. He had only been in Twin Creeks for a few days, and he already knew his prized possession would be a liability here. Maybe he should trade it in for something sturdier, like the lettuce-hauling flatbed that had blocked his path that morning. But no, Joe could never give up that convertible. The sleek luxury sedan wasn't just a car—it was a symbol of everything he had worked so hard for, a reward for the long hours and endless sacrifices. As was the luxury town-home he had rented near the hospital in LA, and the trendy clubs where he easily attracted the attention of beautiful women for a night or two.

Most days his work and play kept him busy and satisfied. But sometimes he felt a strange emptiness tugging at him. A sense that there was something more he was still searching for.

Whatever it was, he sure as hell wasn't going to find it here in Twin Creeks, Montana.

It was impossible to think of the truck without remembering the nurse who drove it. If he were still in LA and he had spotted her in one of the city's trendy clubs, he would have gladly crossed the room to buy her a drink, chat her up and see if he could get something started. He would have shown her the night of her life, then driven her home along the Pacific Coast Highway, feeling the salt and wind against his face as he drove with the top down, racing the waves and the seagulls in sync with whatever music he had blaring on the radio.

Most women he met were looking for what he had to offer. A few nights of glamour and passion, nothing more. And if any woman did get the wrong idea about him, he took her to brunch at his favorite resort where he would gently explain, over quiche and mimosas, that he just wasn't a mortgage-and-minivan kind of guy. Being honest and up-front had allowed him to enjoy the occasional connection he craved without leaving a string of angry, bitter ex-lovers behind.

His casual dating life would probably be one more casualty of this forced exile to Twin Creeks. It was just another handful of salt in the fresh wound of losing his fellowship. But a setback was not destiny, and Twin Creeks was not his forever. So that sweet, midnight-black convertible wasn't going anywhere.

Joe's thoughts drifted back to the ex-nurse he had met that morning. She was a pretty woman with her jet-black hair cut in a short bob. What was her story anyway? She was obviously skilled in trauma care, but she said she wasn't a nurse anymore. What happened? Was she injured? In some kind of professional trouble? That was hard to imagine. She didn't seem the type.

He had looked for her after handing Grace over to the EMTs. But by the time Edith had finished hugging and kissing him and declaring him a *hero* to anyone who would listen, the nurse in the bright pink wool hat with the white tassel was long gone. He hadn't even gotten her name.

"Take the snowmobile, then," the mayor bellowed.

"The what?"

"The snowmobile. It's in the barn. Just fire her up and zip over to your medical clinic in town for the insulin. You can jet over to Bill's place and be back home in no time."

A shock of electricity rippled down Joe's spine as he realized he had two new things to tackle today. Learning to operate a snowmobile and surviving a blizzard.

Joe pressed his thumb between his eyes where a throbbing headache was ramping up. What the hell was he doing here? He should be in Florida where he belonged, on the fellowship he had sacrificed so much for. Instead, he was here in this crazy place with crazy people who expected crazy things in the middle of a crazy snowstorm.

Hey, now, Chambers. It's not the mayor's fault or Bill Parker's fault that you're here.

Whose fault had it been? That was hard to say. All he knew was that his department chair, whose recommendation he'd needed to get that fellowship, had politely declined to support his application.

Not this time, Joe.

He had been completely stunned by her refusal. And confused. His grades were stellar. He had taken every overtime and on-call shift during his residency. While his peers were living it up over drinks at the off-campus bar, he had been at the medical library, researching the latest treatments and pharmaceuticals for cancer. No medical student had sacrificed more to accomplish their goals than he had. So why on earth did his top mentor lack faith in him?

His mentor had tucked a pencil behind her ear, crossed her arms over her chest.

Tell me your most difficult case this week.

That was easy. He rattled off the health metrics of his thirty-four-year-old patient with a history of Type One diabetes. He went into great detail describing the extent of her rapidly worsening renal function, severe hypertension and episodes of hypoglycemia despite careful insulin management. He listed the medication adjustments he had made and the extensive testing he had ordered.

And what is her name, Dr. Chambers?

He was utterly stumped.

Who does she love? And what is she willing to fight for?

He couldn't believe that after eight years of

hard work and sacrifice, these were the questions that were tripping him up.

His mentor had scooted her chair closer so she could meet Joe's gaze. *Do you know the difference between a good doctor and a great doctor, Joe?*

Normally, he would say being committed, knowing your stuff and working harder than everyone else. But he didn't think those were the answers she was seeking.

Curiosity, Joe. Because when we are curious, we ask questions. When we ask questions, we learn things. We're in the business of treating people, Joe, not diseases. Know your patient, and you'll know their cure.

At that point, she had pushed away from him, scooted her chair back to her desk, then handed him a sheet of paper. She had a twinkle in her eye he had never seen before. "I'd like you to spend some time in Twin Creeks, Joe. It's a small town in western Montana where I grew up. Their long-time doctor has passed away and they need an interim doctor for a few months. It's your choice, of course, but I think you'll find it a special place where you can expand some of your people skills. Go there and come spring, I'll recommend you for the oncology fellowship in Florida."

Joe had questions—so many questions—and lots more fight in him. But she had already turned back to her computer—her way of saying the meeting was over.

Joe thought this was the most idiotic thing his medical training had asked of him. But there wasn't a damn thing he could do about it. Without her blessing, he had zero chance of landing an oncology fellowship anywhere. So after packing all of his worldly possessions into a moving truck, he and Daisy had set off for the west coast drive to Twin Creeks, Montana. Just in time for Winter Storm Isabella.

Joe shook off his frustration and rooted through the kitchen drawer for paper and a pen. "And where will I find Bill Parker?"

"I told you. Blue Sky Valley, just past the widow's place."

Joe's pencil hovered over the paper, waiting for something useful. "I have no idea what that means."

The mayor sighed. "Blue Sky Valley is on the north side of the county, butted up against the mountains. Set your GPS to 46.1263 degrees north and 112.9478 degrees west and you'll be in the general area. Use forest roads when you get out of town. You'll pass a small homestead—that's the widow's place. Keep heading north and stick to the tree line. You'll find Bill's cabin soon enough. If you leave now, you should get back before the storm gets going real good."

Joe glanced out the window at the mess of snow and ice. This was going to get worse?

Joe ignored the feeling of dread coiling in his chest and wrote the directions on his pad. The staffing recruiter had warned him that rural medicine was different from what he was used to. But he thought that meant less access to specialists and hospitals, fewer resources. He hadn't counted on doing house calls on a snowmobile in blizzard conditions.

Joe hung up, shrugged on his jacket and went out to the small barn that flanked his rented home. Daisy followed close at his heels.

He pulled off the snowmobile cover. It was black and sleek with a few dents and scratches from its previous adventures.

"Snowmobiling," Joe said to Daisy. "How hard could it be?"

Daisy yowled and flopped to the floor, dropping her chin to her paws and looking up at him with her soulful brown eyes.

"Oh, who asked you?" Joe muttered. He ran his fingers over the various gauges. The key dangled from the ignition. The left grip was the throttle; right was the brakes.

"See, this isn't so hard," Joe said, as much to himself as to Daisy.

There was also an open box-shaped sled that looked like it could haul a good number of supplies. Maybe even a person. If house calls were going to be part of his job description, a utility sled like this would be pretty handy.

Joe returned to the house to dress in his warmest winter gear and enter the GPS coordinates in his phone. He made a mental note to purchase a rugged, heavy-duty GPS unit as soon as possible. For now, his cell phone would have to do.

Daisy positioned herself between him and the door, her tail wagging wildly like a metronome.

"Not this time, girl. You're safer here."

Daisy threw back her head and yowled in protest. Joe's heart sank. He didn't know how she did it, but Daisy was some kind of expert at reading human emotions. And right now his heart didn't want to leave her behind. Unlike his father, who had found his solace at the bar after his mother died, Daisy had never abandoned him.

Joe crouched to stroke her ear the way she

liked. "Aw, Daisy. You don't want to be alone, do you?"

Daisy tilted her head to rest it in his hand, just as she had with the pretty nurse back at the Shop-and-Go. Cripes, there he went again, thinking about the mysterious nurse. This had to stop. The fellowship application cycle would open again in a few months. If he wanted to get his shot at that fellowship, he needed to trust his head, not his heart. There was something his mentor wanted him to learn here in Twin Creeks, and the mysterious woman at the Shop-and-Go had nothing to do with it.

He could hardly blame Daisy. Everything here was strange for both of them.

"All right, girl, let's go."

Daisy sprang to her feet and glued herself to his hip as he locked the house. Then he hitched the box-freight sled to the snowmobile, layered it with blankets and gave Daisy the command to go. She jumped into the boxy space, spun once and settled into the soft bed he had made for her.

"Stay put," he warned her in his *I mean business* voice. "Even if you see a squirrel!"

So long as he took things nice and slow, they should be fine. But he had to be careful. Sometimes he revved the throttle when he meant to use the brake, resulting in a frightening surge forward.

Joe found the supply of insulin in the refrigerator at the clinic where he would start seeing patients in a few days. He was settling Daisy back in the sled when his cell phone rang. Joe checked the screen, desperately hoping it might be the mayor telling him to never mind, Bill had found extra insulin at home so Joe could go back to bed. But he had no such luck. It was his father's photo on the screen.

Joe studied his father's image. Recovery looked good on him. He was no longer the man Joe remembered from his youth, overwhelmed by grief and parenthood. Back then, he had found his solace in working far too much, then stopping at the bar for a "bite to eat" on the way home. Which turned into a pint…or four. As a father, he did most of what he was supposed to do. He made sure the house was stocked with food and that Joe's homework was done. *High-functioning alcoholism* they called it. But emotionally, he was long gone, drowning in grief after losing his wife just two months after she was diagnosed with ovarian cancer.

Joe sent the call to voice mail. He knew what his father was calling about and he didn't want to talk about it again. He had no intention of taking the newly developed test that would determine if he carried the same gene that had caused his mother and four other relatives to develop cancer before their fiftieth birthday. He knew his father loved him and was worried for him, but what was the point? Knowing he carried the gene only meant he would be screened more often and aggressively. It didn't mean he could beat his genetic fate.

So he'd decided long ago that he would rather not know. It was better to throw himself into a career of fighting cancer. It was too late to help his family, but maybe he could help others. Maybe he could be the doctor his family had needed in their darkest hour.

And it was why he wasn't a mortgage-and-minivan kind of guy. He had no intention of ever having a serious relationship. Losing his mother had almost destroyed his father and left him with memories of a dark and lonely childhood. It wasn't fair to let someone fall in love with him, knowing that one day they would have to watch him prematurely grow sick and die. And he sure as hell wasn't going to knowingly pass these genes on to an innocent child.

So there would be no love, no wedding bells, no tiny feet pitter-pattering through his

home. He loved his work, and he loved Daisy…
period. Most days, he was happy enough. And
if he felt a little lonely from time to time, well,
that was just the cost of doing the right thing.

Joe tucked his phone into his pocket, then
settled Daisy back in the sled. He kept the pace
nice and slow all the way to Bill's cabin, making sure to check his bearings often on the GPS
app to ensure he was still on course. It was impossible to tell with the low visibility.

By the time they were ready to head back
home, both he and Daisy were wet and miser-
able from the snow and wind. They were on
a well-marked forest trail now, which made
him feel a little more confident of his bearings.
Thoughts of getting back to his warm house
and starting a crackling fire spurred him on,
making him a little more reckless.

He revved the throttle, taking the snowmobile up to thirty mph, then forty. At this speed,
they would be home in no time.

Up ahead there was a curve in the trail,
marked by a thicket of trees and some huge
boulders. Joe reduced the throttle to slow the
snowmobile for the curve.

But a rough patch in the ice-covered trail
startled him. Instead of braking, he hit the
throttle…hard.

CHAPTER THREE

"I'M READY, MOMMY!"

Alexa emerged from her room wearing adorable snowman winter pajamas with a matching robe cinched tight against her little round belly. She had her favorite teddy bear stuffed under her arm.

Lily looked up from the kitchen where she was putting the final touches on their winter snack. "Okay, I've just decided. Five is my favorite age for little girls like you."

"I'm five!" Alexa said, her tone full of wonder.

"Yes, you are." Lily filled a ceramic teapot with homemade hot chocolate, then set it on a serving tray alongside small bowls of marshmallows, peppermint sticks, whipped cream and little snowman cocktail napkins.

The oven timer dinged, signaling that their chunky monkey brownies were ready. Ooey-gooey brownies packed with caramel and white chocolate chips.

This was probably the unhealthiest "dinner" Lily had ever served her daughter, but she wanted to start their snowy retreat off right. There would be plenty of time to make Alexa eat her veggies later.

For now, they still had power, so they planned to watch their first holiday movie of the season with this carb-centric snack. Later, when the power was out, they would rely on the fireplace for heat and the generator to keep the refrigerator and lights on. That was when they would switch to the healthy granola bars Lily had baked, along with strawberry smoothies that had a secret handful of spinach blended in.

Alexa plopped herself on the couch and patted the spot next to her. "Come sit by me, Mommy!"

"Just where I want to be!" One of the many nonsense rhymes they had created over the five years of being a family of two.

Oh, it was so nice to have this time with her. For the first few years in Copper Ridge, Lily had been able to survive on Connor's small life insurance policy. Getting a part-time, work-from-home job with a nursing journal was the perfect way to help the insurance money last longer while still filling Alexa's days with nature hikes and library trips. Lily knew she probably tried too hard to make up for Alexa's not having a father.

Lily had let Alexa pick out any movies she wanted from the library's holiday collection. Just a few minutes into the film, she realized that might have been a mistake.

Because this movie featured a class of first graders who did a silly science experiment with a snowman in their playground, then discovered that they accidentally brought him to life. Mayhem and misadventure ensued.

It was a cute and charming story that had Alexa mesmerized. But Lily gritted her teeth and sipped her hot chocolate, desperately hoping that Alexa would just enjoy the story and not focus too much on…

"I want to go to school," Alexa said suddenly and with great determination. "Like those kids."

"Well, you will go to school. Even if we decide to homeschool, there's lots of classes we can take at the library."

"Not like that!" Alexa was adamant. "I want to go to a school like them." She pointed to the television. "With a teacher, and a classroom, and recess and everything!"

This was Alexa's last winter attending a home-based preschool in their neighborhood. The following fall, she would be old enough to board the yellow bus that drove by their house every morning and afternoon.

Oh, gosh, she didn't want to argue with Alexa. Not now, when everything was starting so well. Maybe a little distraction was in order.

"You know what we forgot? The popcorn!"

Lily headed to the kitchen and filled the popcorn machine with kernels. She slid a bowl under the chute, then snuck a peek into the living room. Alexa was busy examining the rock-painting kit that Lily had brought home from the Shop-n-Go. If Lily waited just a little bit longer, Alexa might focus on rock painting instead of kindergarten, giving them a much-needed peaceful evening.

Lily glanced out the window. It was snowing quite hard now. Not quite whiteout conditions, but close. She grabbed her sweater from a hook near the back door and went outside to the screened-in porch, then flipped on her porch light so she could watch the beauty of a powerful winter storm.

The storm was picking up momentum now. Snow fell steady and hard, covering her house and driveway in a thick white blanket.

She shivered as wind whistled through the screened-in porch, chilling her to the bone.

Her thoughts turned to Grace. She had called the hospital twice since she got back from the Shop-n-Go and was heartened to hear that Grace was in critical but stable condition. She involuntarily shuddered as she remembered how close Grace had come to dying. If it hadn't been for Joe Chambers, who knows what might have happened?

"Joe Chambers..." She whispered his name out loud and it tasted like candy.

Lily wasn't prone to infatuations, but she couldn't quite put memories of her encounter with the sexy stranger to rest. Jennifer, her good friend and landlord, would be thrilled. She had started working on Lily a year or two after she moved to Twin Creeks.

You're a young, beautiful woman, sweetie, she had said. *You deserve to be looked after, you know?*

People kept telling her that she needed to find closure, move on, that sort of thing. Lily didn't know—maybe Jennifer was right. So she'd tried. She hired a sitter to go out with the men Jennifer had thought would be just perfect for her. Her dates had been nice enough, and she couldn't deny it felt good to enjoy some attention and laughs over dinner and wine.

But she'd known soon enough that she could never go beyond dinner. Her heart had barely survived the loss of Connor. How could she ever let herself fall in love again, knowing that at any moment, some random act of fate could snatch it all away? Even if she wanted to fall in love again, she couldn't risk breaking Alexa's heart, too, if love wasn't going to stay.

Jennifer had been disappointed when Lily told her there would be no more dates.

I understand, she told Lily, giving her arm an affectionate squeeze. *But honey, sometimes love finds us, whether we're ready or not.*

That had been the end of her dating life. That is, until today. Ugh, there it was again. The image of Joe braced against the grocery store shelf, flashing her that brilliant smile as they pointlessly bantered about a parking space. He'd been flirting with her and damn if she hadn't liked it…a lot.

Who was he anyway? His out-of-state plates made winter tourist seem likely, but he didn't have a ski rack mounted to his car roof and he didn't look like a hunter. He was probably just passing through Twin Creeks on his way to the bigger city of Billings. Which was for the best, really. She might be lonely from time to time, but being lonely was better than being heartbroken.

She'd feel a lot less lonely if she could stop thinking about Joe Chambers and his perfect jawline. She left the shelter of her porch and stepped out into the storm. She wanted to feel the wind and ice battering her body instead of the loneliness making her heart ache.

She was instantly pelted by snow and tiny ice shards. The wind howled through the courtyard between her little cottage and the main house. Snow and ice chafed her cheeks and made her eyes sting.

She closed her eyes against the storm and realized that if she tilted her head just right, the wind howling through the ponderosa pines sounded a little like the blades of an emergency rescue helicopter. It was enough to conjure memories of rescue calls from long ago.

Loma Linda base, this is Medevac 2646...

Medevac 2646, on call out to Apple Valley...

Medevac 2646, requesting space in your emergency room...

Patient with positive LOC...

Patient with a fractured left ankle...

Even though it was five years ago, she could still remember so many patients. Their names and faces. The accidents and injuries. Their fear and pain.

She missed that job *so* much. She missed being there for people at their darkest hour. Holding their hand as they crossed the city skies, far above the bustling city that had its own problems and worries. In every call, she strived to be the beacon of hope someone needed when their entire world had crashed around them.

The wind was whipping into a frenzy now. Soon, they would be in whiteout conditions. She was chilled to the bone but didn't want to leave. It felt too good to imagine herself back in the action and thrill of her former work as a flight nurse.

Medevac 2646, we have a patient with partial facial paralysis...

"Help...we need help!"

This is Medevac 2646...recommend that the orthopedic team be on standby...

"Help me! Please! Can you please help me?"

At first, she thought the cries for help were part of her memories. But when she opened her eyes, she could still hear the cries.

The cries were very faint, just barely audible in between the howling wind gusts.

She waited; her head cocked…yes! There it was. Someone was crying out for help.

She ran inside and turned on the switches for her exterior lighting around the barn.

There, off in the distance, she could see something moving toward the farm. The barest impression of a dark shape headed her way.

"What is it, Mommy?" Alexa joined her at the back door, her brow furrowed with worry.

"I don't know, baby. I think someone might need our help."

She didn't even know that for sure. But her trauma rescue skills were kicking in, and she felt a familiar surge of adrenaline for the second time that day.

She dashed to the hallway closet, donning her heavy winter coat and boots, then slammed on her gloves and winter hat before heading for the door.

"I'll come, too, Mommy!" Alexa trailed after her mother, her teddy bear dragging behind her.

"No, baby—you're not dressed warm enough. Stay here in the kitchen. I'm just going to take a look."

Lily grabbed her most powerful flashlight, kissed Alexa's cheek and went outdoors.

At first, she couldn't see a damn thing.

Nothing but snow flurries and pitch-black night. She strained to hear the voice calling for help again, but the howling winds were no match for a human voice. After several long and cold minutes, she was starting to think she had imagined everything. But somehow it felt wrong to give up and go back indoors, even though the wind was practically pushing her that way.

Then she saw the figure moving between the barn and house. She couldn't tell what it was exactly, but it was definitely not her imagination.

She ran off the porch to the figure. It was a man, stumbling through the thick snow, cradling one arm with the other.

If he was yelling before, he wasn't yelling anymore. Maybe he was too tired or weak, or maybe it was because he got a mouthful of snow every time he tried.

She caught up to him and gripped his arm. "It's okay!" she shouted. "You made it!"

He looked up at her, startled, as if he didn't expect his cries to actually rally help. His eyebrows and lashes were frosted with snow. He had a flannel scarf wrapped tight around his face, so all she could see was his eyes. Eyes that were very familiar.

Lily tugged at his arm. "Let's get you inside!" she shouted.

But he resisted her pull, shouting something that was hard to understand between his scarf and the wind. Something about a snowmobile…an accident…

"I don't understand!" she yelled.

He pulled down his scarf and shouted as hard as he could. "Daisy…! Injured…" He gestured wildly at the direction that he'd come from.

Under the lamplight, with his scarf removed, she could see why his eyes seemed familiar.

It was Joe Chambers. From the Shop-n-Go!

Her heart fluttered for a moment, stunned to see him here in her courtyard. Had she somehow managed to conjure him into her life with her incessant thoughts of him all afternoon?

"Daisy?" she screamed back, remembering the sweet dog who had befriended her in the store.

"Yes! Have to…help her!" He pointed to his arm and then she understood. He was too injured to help Daisy on his own.

He gestured for her to follow him, but there was no way they could just jet off into the night in the middle of a blizzard. They would end up lost or injured for sure.

And she couldn't leave little Alexa here all by herself.

Joe had already turned back in the direction he came from. She grabbed his arm and hauled him back.

"We need supplies!" she shouted, hoping he could hear at least half of what she said. "Come with me!"

He looked behind him, where he had left Daisy, and then to her cabin with its brightly illuminated windows and warm, crackling fire.

The look on his face was pure anguish.

He was stuck; she could see that. Stuck between doing *something* to help Daisy, even if it got him killed, and following her.

She needed him to trust her if they were going to help Daisy. The same way she had needed her trauma patients to trust her before she strapped them into a helicopter and whisked them off to unknown places.

So she told him what she had told her patients. "Everything's going to be okay, Joe. I will make sure of that."

Lily swung the cabin door open with a crash and waved Joe inside. "Come in, come in!" she gushed.

Joe was nearly frozen numb from all the time

he'd spent in the fierce winter storm. First, on the snowmobile trip to Bill, then spending who knows how long stumbling through the snow, hoping against all odds that he might catch a glimpse of lights from the tiny cabin he had passed earlier.

He stood just inside the doorway, still mystified that he had managed to make it here safely. The woman pulled off her pink winter hat with the white tassel. The same hat she had worn that morning when he first saw her at the Shop-n-Go. Then she slipped out of her boots covered in slush and put on a pair of slippers shaped like soft white bunnies.

She disappeared for a moment, then returned with a mug of hot coffee and a few rolls of bandage wraps. "What happened?"

Joe didn't know if she meant the throbbing arm he had pressed protectively against his side or what brought him to her doorstep. "Snowmobile accident," he managed to get out, because that would answer both questions.

It was warm in the foyer. Warm enough that his teeth had stopped chattering though he still felt frozen to the core. The unmistakable aroma of something hot and delicious wafted from the kitchen, making his mouth water against his will.

"And you had Daisy with you?"

Hearing it from her lips made it sound completely ridiculous. Reckless even. But he lacked the energy to explain the whole story, so he just nodded.

"Where is she now?"

"Pinned under the snowmobile. It flipped when I took the corner too fast. She was in an attached trailer, but somehow she ended up pinned under the snow machine. I tried, but I couldn't lift it." He indicated his injured arm with a frustrated shrug.

Then she was right in front of him, the mysterious woman from the Shop-n-Go. For a moment, he thought she might hug him. But no, she was looping something over his head. It was a makeshift sling she had created with the bandage wrap. She held it open wide so he could wriggle his arm inside. That small motion was enough to launch another explosion of fireworks deep in his shoulder and neck, but then she wrapped his arm snug against his body. The combination of support and stabilization provided a small measure of comfort.

"Here, take these." She offered him two orange pills from her pocket. "We'll check you out later, after we've found Daisy. Until then, hopefully these will help your pain a bit."

He swallowed the pills dry. They were just garden-variety anti-inflammatories sold at any drugstore. He doubted they would do much to combat the ripping, searing sensation in his shoulder, but he appreciated her effort all the same.

She patted his good arm gently. "I've got to gather a few things before we leave. Why don't you come into the kitchen and have some soup. It'll do you some good to warm up before we go find Daisy."

Joe shook his head in confusion. The warm house, hot coffee, homemade soup, soft bunny slippers—these were the trappings that came with a normal day. But today wasn't normal. It was a disaster, and it was all his fault.

He started to protest but it was as if she could read his mind. "Everything will be okay. But it could be a long night. Leave your jacket and boots here—we'll get you fixed up with something to eat."

He followed her to the kitchen and went on autopilot, sitting on the chair she pulled out for him and accepting the bowl of soup. Until that moment, he'd been functioning from a comfortably numb place. Just doing what he had to do, moment by moment, to survive his ordeal. But the heat of the ceramic bowl, the fragrant steam of the soup, the tantalizing aroma of basil and tomato broth with hunks of hearty stew meat—its simple pleasure was almost overwhelming.

She smiled at his expression. "Like it? It's a family recipe." She dropped into the chair next to him. "I'm Lily, by the way."

"I remember you from the Shop-n-Go this morning."

"I recognized you, too." He wondered how, with his face all bundled up against the snow and cold.

That was all he could manage. The heat and aroma of the soup was getting to him. She had served it in a blue ceramic bowl with a slab of what appeared to be homemade bread. And a glass of cold milk.

Just a few bites, he told himself. *Then I'll insist we get going.*

But the first bite completely felled him. Stew beef, root vegetables and a thick, satisfying broth utterly did him in. Once he took that first bite, he could not stop. He devoured bite after delicious bite while Lily quizzed him on his journey, trying to get a bearing on where he had crashed. He knew he had been on a forest service road, following the route based on his GPS directions. He described the landmarks he had passed, including her cabin, before the accident.

"I think I know where Daisy is," she said, her brow furrowed in thought. Then she jumped to her feet. "I'll be right back. I need to ask my landlord to stay with Alexa."

She disappeared, leaving him to wonder who Alexa was. He was more concerned with scraping the last drops of broth from the bowl. He was so engrossed that he didn't notice a little scrap of a girl standing by his elbow, her expression quite solemn.

"Hello," he said. "You must be Alexa."

She neither confirmed nor denied his assumption. Instead, she blinked twice. "Mommy says your doggie is hurt."

"That's true. She's trapped in the snow, but your mom and dad are going to help me rescue her."

The girl gave him a funny little frown. "Daddy can't help."

"No?"

She shook her head hard, making her auburn curls shimmy and shake. "He's with the angels now."

"Oh." Joe's heart squeezed with sympathy. He had been older than Alexa when his mother had died of cancer. Old enough to understand, but not old enough to accept the feckless, random hand of fate. He didn't know if he would ever be old enough to accept the *c'est la vie* canned advice that some people doled out in the face of incomprehensible loss.

He put his hand over his heart. "Ouch," he told the little girl with the big brown eyes. Because what else could he say that would let her know he understood? She nodded in return, as if she understood him perfectly.

Lily returned, her arms full of supplies, and dumped them on the table. A topo map and GPS unit. Water bottles, ski goggles, flashlights, medical supplies, headlamps and a handful of granola bars.

"Jennifer's on her way," Lily told Alexa.

Alexa groaned and dropped into the chair next to Joe. "Aww, I want to come, too!"

"'Fraid not, kitten. The weather's too rough. You'll be safe here with Jennifer—I'll be back in a jiffy!"

Joe stood so he could return to the foyer and put his boots and jacket back on. He'd lost track of time since he'd come to Lily's cabin, but it felt like too long. Every minute in her safe, warm home was one more minute that Daisy was alone, cold and afraid.

Lily bit her lip. "I just need one more thing from the shed."

Joe's heart sank. He could understand Lily's need to find someone to stay with her daughter, but with that taken care of, he wanted—no, he *needed* to get back in the storm and find Daisy.

She must have read his expression because she paused, her hand on the doorknob. "I'll be quick, Joe. I promise."

And then she was gone. He watched helplessly through the paned window as her dark figure crossed the open courtyard between her little cabin and the barn that was illuminated by the exterior floodlights. She was so small and the storm so ferocious that he momentarily feared she would get lost, too; swallowed up by a storm that seemed intent on obliterating everything in its path.

He wanted to scream with frustration, but Alexa had joined him in the foyer, and he didn't want to scare her, too.

"What's your doggie's name?"

He dropped to the bench, then winced at the bolt of red-hot pain that zipped from his shoulder down his arm at the sudden movement. "Daisy," he said through gritted teeth.

Alexa spied his wool cap on the bench next

to Lily's pink one. She picked it up, then carefully climbed on top of the bench so she could reach his head and tug his hat down over his ears, though it felt wildly askew. It was cute how she bit her bottom lip when she concentrated. Just like her mother, he realized, when she had been counting his chest compressions on Grace before she gave a deep, hard breath.

He waited until Alexa wasn't looking to straighten his cap. Just then, Lily burst back through the door, a shovel in one hand.

A shovel? Why the hell did she need a shovel? All they needed to do was find Daisy and lift the snowmobile away from her.

Unless Lily thought that Daisy might be beyond rescue?

The lump that formed in his throat was enormous. He forced the terrible image far from his mind. Daisy was going to be fine. She had to be.

She slipped her winter gear back on, leaving those memorable white bunny slippers in the foyer, then helped him back into his winter gear, too. This time she left his injured arm close to his body and just zipped up his jacket, leaving the empty sleeve dangling at his side. After loading their gear onto a sled, she gave Jennifer a hug to thank her for staying with her daughter. Alexa got a quick kiss on the cheek and off they went, abandoning the safety and warmth of Lily's little cabin to head back into the raging storm.

CHAPTER FOUR

As SOON AS they left Lily's screened-in porch, the icy wind snatched away all the warmth and coziness of Lily's warm cabin. But that was okay. All Joe wanted was to get back to his best friend.

Lily led the way, creating deep depressions in the snow that he could follow to conserve his energy. The stress of his injury plus exposure from being outdoors made him the weaker partner.

At first, it felt like Lily was leading them farther away from where he felt the crash site was. But then he saw her logic. By sticking to the tree line, they had some perspective of the landscape despite the poor visibility from the blizzard. And when the path suddenly became an open corridor in the forest with yellow blazes tacked into the trees, he knew she had led them back to the forest road he had traveled before the accident.

Joe felt a sudden surge of energy when he recognized his bearings. So much so that he stopped following her tracks so he could walk alongside her. He couldn't see much of her profile with her yellow goggles and her face wrapped tight with a thick winter scarf. But she gave him a single curt nod to acknowledge him, and he felt like there was intention in that gesture. That whatever happened next, he wouldn't face it alone.

Despite the poor visibility, Joe could just make out the clump of trees that he had passed seconds before the snowmobile crash. He tugged on Lily's arm and pointed toward the field. The wind was too strong to even attempt to speak. She nodded and gave him a thumbs-up. Their pace quickened as they passed the trees. It was then that he could just barely discern lumps in the snow—the boulders! His heart soared with hope. This *was* the crash site. He was sure of it!

All his exhaustion disappeared as he broke into a run, searching for the snowmobile. There! Off in the distance he saw twin beams of light—the lights of his snowmobile were still glowing, thank goodness.

He ran awkwardly through the snow, every jostle making his arm howl with pain. The thick, fresh-fallen snow seemed intent on grabbing him with every step. Still, there wasn't anything that was going to stop him from getting to Daisy.

He cleared the snow machine and dropped to his knees. Daisy was right where he left her, but now she was almost entirely covered with snow. Her head and muzzle remained visible, probably because she kept shaking it off for as long as she could.

But she wasn't moving. And her eyes were closed.

No. No, she couldn't be.

Before he could register that terrible thought, Lily's pink-gloved hands began sweeping snow away from Daisy's muzzle and body. She whipped her goggles off and threw them aside, laser-focused on clearing the pup's airway. Then she cupped her hands around Daisy's muzzle and blew hard, until Joe could see Daisy's chest rise in response.

No, no, no! We're too late!

But Lily didn't seem to think so. She kept repeating the breaths over and over.

"We need to get this damn snowmobile off of her!" Joe screamed, having no idea if Lily could even hear him with the wind howling through the ponderosa pines.

She nodded. Joe struggled to his feet, hoping to rock the snow machine away from Daisy with his one good arm. But before he could try, Lily grabbed him. She pointed to where the machine had landed—on a small outcrop of tree roots that were preventing the full weight of the snow machine from landing on Daisy's body. She was pinned but not crushed.

"Too! Much! Ice!" she screamed, pointing at the ground. He saw her point. Messing with the snowmobile could send it skittering off in the wrong direction.

She grabbed the shovel from her backpack and returned to Daisy, then began digging. He immediately understood her plan. If they dug out enough space from under her body, they could slide her out instead of trying to lift the machine off her. It would be safer and faster.

And it would never have been an option if Lily hadn't insisted on bringing the shovel.

Joe dropped to his knees and began digging at the snow with his one exposed hand. Soon, they had cleared a deep depression under her body.

Lily looked at him, her brown eyes calm and focused. "Ready?"

He read her lips more than heard her words, and he nodded. He held Daisy's head steady with his good arm while Lily braced Daisy's body with her hands.

"One! Two! Three!" she screamed.

Together they guided Daisy's body away from the snow machine. The sudden motion made the machine lose its precarious balance and crash-land into the space where Daisy's body had just been.

Joe felt a sudden, sickening wave of nausea roil his gut at the thought of how close Daisy had been to disaster.

But there was no time to think about that.

Joe grabbed the sled with his good arm and arranged the blankets into a makeshift bed. As Lily lifted Daisy's body, she gave a soft little whimper that made Joe's heart soar. She was alive! Not in great shape, but alive! They worked together to cover Daisy with more blankets, then improvised a safety strap system using the extra bandage wraps Lily had packed.

His fingers were numb to the bone, but he just had to rub Daisy's ear the way she liked. Lily slipped her goggles and gloves back on, then pointed at the trail. He got the message loud and clear.

Let's get the hell out of here.

She grabbed the sled pull and he followed

behind, his heart in his throat. Lily had thought of everything they might need out here, while he had just wanted to bolt out the door. If they had followed his instincts instead of hers, they might still be searching for the crash site.

He felt greatly humbled by this terrible day. All he had wanted when he accepted the temporary job as town doctor was to escape the humiliation and shame of losing his fellowship after years of hard work. He thought Montana would be a refuge and a reprieve. A place he could hide away until his mentor deemed him ready for the Florida fellowship program.

But Montana was nothing like California. And if he didn't figure things out here pretty quick, he could get himself or someone else killed.

He kept his eyes on the determined woman leading the way back to safety. She didn't even know him, yet she had jumped in with both feet when he needed help. Unlike him, she knew what she was doing.

I used to be a flight nurse...a long time ago...

There had been sadness in her face when she said that. He had no doubt that she must have been a spectacular flight nurse. She was calm under pressure, had quick planning skills and was determined and focused.

All qualities that a medical professional working in this rural, wild place needed to be successful.

His mentor had told him that the state wanted to recruit more doctors and nurses to their rural communities. He even had a budget to add a nurse and a medical technician to his downtown medical clinic. But no one seemed to want to relocate to a rural area like Twin Creeks, so the towns had to rely on traveling doctors and nurses to rotate through on a monthly basis.

That lack of medical care was dangerous for the farmers and ranchers who worked the land. People put off seeing a doctor because the closest city was a hundred miles away. Small problems became life-threatening ones, and emergency care was sketchy at best.

Yet, Lily lived right here and clearly had top-notch skills and could work under challenging conditions. So why wasn't she working at the clinic?

It was flat-out none of his business. Maybe she'd had a workplace injury. Or some kind of professional trouble.

Whatever the reason, it was none...of... his...damn...business.

I used to be a flight nurse... Those sad brown eyes. *But that was a long time ago.*

It wasn't just a matter of curiosity anymore. This town needed her.

And maybe he needed her, too.

Lily quietly closed the door to her daughter's bedroom. Alexa was totally exhausted after spending the evening tending to Daisy like a little mother.

Somehow, despite the accident and her exposure to the cold, Daisy seemed to have survived her accident unscathed. Lily had called the town's sole veterinarian who guided her through the basics of a veterinary exam. Daisy was resting now, curled in front of the fire on a pile of blankets that Alexa had fluffed into a little bed. Though her eyes were shut tight, she had kept one ear cocked in Joe's direction all evening, opening her eyes only if Joe moved or coughed. All things considered, Daisy was a very lucky dog.

Lily paused before descending the stairs. Joe sat where she'd left him, on the couch with amber light from the fire casting dancing shadows across his face. Her coffee table was strewn with plates, mugs and playing cards from where they had played games with Alexa after dinner.

Joe was engrossed in his phone, so it took a

moment for him to notice her return, affording her a long look at his profile. He had an excellent nose, she thought, narrow and straight, and a broad, smooth forehead. His flannel shirt was unbuttoned at the neck, revealing a strong throat and a glimpse of his smooth, athletic chest.

Her body thrilled at the sight of this man in her living room. It had been just her and Alexa for so long. Not that their tiny family wasn't enough. She had everything she needed for a lifetime of happiness—a safe, dry home, a few good friends and a bright, healthy daughter. She had never felt any lack in her new life in Twin Creeks.

And yet… Joe's masculine energy was stirring something in her that she thought had died long ago. It was like realizing that cake was pretty good, but cake with icing… Well, that was a tempting, decadent treat. She wasn't sure if this was good or not. On the one hand, it meant she was still alive. A healthy, vibrant woman with robust sexual appetites. But it felt dangerous, too. Like opening a Pandora's Box of forbidden desires that could trample her fragile life if she surrendered. She swallowed hard, straightened her sweater and joined him in the living room.

He looked up from his phone with a furrowed brow. "I think you have to restart your router. I can't get internet access."

Lily cast her gaze to the window where the blizzard continued to rage. "Yeah, I don't think it's the router."

Joe's eyes widened. "So, no internet until tomorrow?"

She nibbled the edge of her nail, a nervous habit she couldn't quite give up. "Or the next day."

"You've got to be kidding. How the heck do you function without internet service for two days?"

She laughed at his incredulous expression. "The same way people functioned before the internet existed. Chores, books, baking…we even take a hike once in a while."

Joe held up a weary hand. "Stop. You're making me tired just thinking about all that."

"Speaking of tired," she said, noticing how the tiny muscles around his eyes were tensed, the hitch of his shoulders. Joe was in more pain than he was letting on. "Looks like you could use a rest yourself. And another dose of pain meds?"

"That would be great." He lifted his mug.

"And maybe something a little stronger than hot chocolate?"

Lily swiftly cleared the coffee table of plates and cups, then returned with two crystal tumblers filled with ice and a bottle of single-malt whiskey. It was a farewell gift from her trauma team when she'd left Chicago.

Save it for a special occasion, her boss had told her. A historic blizzard and her surprise visitor certainly qualified.

Joe had gathered the cards and was shuffling them one-handed as he gazed into the fire. There was an awkward moment as she considered where to sit. There was a chair opposite the couch, but it was far enough that it felt distant and rude. She opted to join him on the couch, putting him within arm's length. Which felt a lot different than when it had been the three of them playing cards and board games all evening.

He smiled as she sat down and waggled the cards in his hand. "Up for another round of Go Fish?"

She wrinkled her nose. "Nah, let's play something more grown-up. How 'bout poker?"

She plucked the card deck from his hand. The fire was going, making the room quite warm and cozy. The candles and camping lanterns she had set out when the power went out added a hazy warm glow to the room.

She counted out five cards for both of them. "So, Dr. Joe Chambers. You just passing through our little town or will you be staying a while?"

"Both, I suppose. I just completed my residency training in Los Angeles and I had hoped to start an oncology fellowship this winter. But my mentor—" Joe took a sip of his whiskey "—strongly encouraged me to spend some time in Twin Creeks, serving as the interim doctor until a permanent replacement is hired."

"Oh," she said. "I wonder how she knew we needed an interim doctor? I thought the town was planning to rely on traveling doctors for now."

"She said she grew up here. She called Twin Creeks a *special place*."

Lily smiled at the description of her quirky new hometown. "That it is. But I wonder why she thought Twin Creeks would be good preparation for an oncology career? We don't have any cancer treatment centers here."

"I think she wanted me to have the opportunity to…get a little more life experience." He shifted in his seat, his jaw tight and his words clipped, clearly uncomfortable and frustrated with the details he was sharing.

Lily had no idea why his mentor would send him to their tiny town for more life experience. But clearly, Joe wasn't happy about it. "I'd say you're off to a good start," Lily said, hoping to turn the conversation back to easier topics.

"How's that?"

"You have life experience with a blizzard now."

He chuckled wearily. "I guess that's true."

Lily tried to keep her focus on the cards in her hand and not on the gorgeous man next to her. But the firelight played against his angular features, and it was hard to ignore the soapy fresh scent of his aftershave. She took a deep, bracing breath to steady herself.

"We don't have any poker chips," she said apologetically. "Hold on." She stretched to reach the baskets where she stored Alexa's small toys below her TV cabinet. She found a handful of plastic safari animals and dropped them on the coffee table.

Joe laughed. "A bit unconventional, but okay. I propose an opening bet of two tigers."

"I'll see your two tigers and raise you one camel and one hippo."

"Am I being hustled here?" he fake groused.

She laughed but felt the heat in her cheeks rise as she caught his gaze lingering on her features. Electric tingles of anticipation zipped up and down her spine. She was so out of practice with socializing with someone new. Especially someone who looked like him.

Joe checked the cards in his hand, then threw two bears into the pile. "So how long have you been in Twin Creeks?"

She matched his bears with two of her own, then tucked a wayward strand of hair behind her ears. "I moved here five years ago from Chicago. Alexa was just an infant."

"So, you left Chicago for—" he gestured to the window where Isabella raged on "—this paradise?"

She made a face at him. "Twin Creeks isn't that bad. You've just got to give it a chance."

"I *am* giving Twin Creeks a chance. Just long enough for a new doc to be hired."

She liked his mischievous smile. After considering her hand, she took another card from the pile. "I don't know, Doc. Twin Creeks just might grow on you."

"Like a fungus? There's medication for that, you know."

Joe leaned back into the couch and stretched his arms across its length. Lily was suddenly very aware of how close he was. If she leaned back, too, his arm would brush her shoulders.

"Seriously, how did you get here? Did you lose a bet? Owe someone money in Chicago?"

She smiled and tucked a strand of hair behind her ear. "My husband and I used to ski here every winter. He died shortly after I found out I was pregnant with Alexa. When Jennifer heard, she insisted I stay in her vacation rental for as long as I liked. But once I got here," she said, shrugging, "I didn't want to leave."

Joe sat in quiet contemplation, his brow slightly furrowed as he listened.

She looked around her cabin. The mantel over the fireplace was filled with framed pictures of her, Connor and Alexa—but none of them together as a family. One corner of her tiny living room was filled with a miniature-size kitchen where Alexa spent hours preparing snacks and meals for her stuffed animals. The bookshelves were stuffed with books and puzzles, and a basket near the fireplace overflowed with soft blankets for her and Alexa's nightly snuggle sessions.

"I think everything worked out okay. As okay as they can be considering our circumstances."

Joe regarded her for a long minute before

setting his whiskey on the coffee table. "At the Shop-n-Go, you said you used to be a flight trauma nurse. What do you do now?"

"I was a nurse practitioner, actually. Now I'm a writer and editor for a medical journal about emergency nursing."

"Big change from jumping out of helicopters and keeping critically injured patients alive."

True, but there were no abusive husbands here, armed and angry. The only threat she had to worry about was whether her internet access would last long enough to get her articles uploaded by their deadline. "Yeah, that's true. But I'm able to work from home. It's great."

"*Great* like this is your dream job or *great* like it keeps the bills paid?"

He was looking at her in a way that made her feel a little too seen. She bit her lip and looked away. "Bill paying is important."

"No doubt about that. But would you ever…" He trailed off, then snapped his mouth shut and gazed down at his drink.

"What?" she prompted, now curious.

He shook his head and shifted his weight away from her. "Nothing, sorry. I'm just glad you found a good place to land when you needed it." He reached to set his glass on the table, the sudden motion making him wince with pain.

Lily noticed. "All right, Joe. Let me check out that shoulder."

CHAPTER FIVE

IT WAS REFLEXIVE, really, his urge to wave her off and swear he felt fine. After years of his father being emotionally absent, he had learned not to draw attention to himself. What was the point? There wasn't anyone around to care.

But his shoulder was starting to ache like crazy despite the painkillers she'd given him. He didn't know what she could do for him out in the middle of nowhere, but she was right. Getting some sense of what might be wrong was a good start.

She leaned into his space until she was close enough that he could smell the soap from her recent shower mixed with nutmeg and cloves from the kitchen. Her hands were gentle as she helped extricate his arm from the sling.

"Extend your arm. Thumb down, please."

He tried to follow her directions, but the pressure of her soft, cool hand against his arm was incredibly distracting. Maybe she was better medicine than those little orange pills. He forced himself to concentrate on her words.

"Does this hurt, Joe?"

Heavens, it hurt a lot, but he didn't want her to stop touching him.

"Sorry about that. Can you raise your arm straight up and then lower it slowly?"

He gave it a try, his gaze lingering on her lovely mouth as she spoke. The upward motion wasn't too bad, but when he tried to lower the arm slowly, his shoulder just completely gave out and he felt a sudden shredding sensation with a lightning bolt of intense pain. He cried out before he could stop himself, pulling his arm into his body for protection.

"Oh, no, I'm so sorry!"

The waves of pain rocked him to the core but even that couldn't distract him from how she curved her hand over his knee. "I didn't mean to hurt you. Here, may I?"

She leaned into his space with outstretched hands, and he wasn't sure what she wanted. But she was so beautiful and earnest as her smoky brown eyes studied his face. She had the cutest pointy nose and a sharp little chin that jutted just so. It was impossible to imagine any request she could make that he wouldn't move heaven and earth to grant her. But at that moment, with the deep ache in his shoulder, all he could manage was a nod.

She reached for him, her hands hesitating at his collar. He watched, mesmerized, as her tongue darted to lick her lips before she unbuttoned the top button of his shirt, then the next and the next. She glanced up to catch his gaze, then gave him a tentative smile. Using his knee for leverage, she pushed herself off the floor, then sat on the couch behind him.

He felt the light brush of her hip against his shoulder, her hands slipping under his shirt. Light as a feather, she carefully slipped his shirt off his shoulder. The cool air of the cabin wafted over his skin, chilling him, but he knew the goose bumps that prickled his flesh weren't from that. It was from her—the thrill of her leg against his shoulder, the softness of her hands sliding across his skin. Her fingers were gentle but probing and he knew she was searching for signs of dislocation or a fracture. But all he could think about was how good her touch felt as her fingers swooped and glided over his skin. The intoxicating blend of her touch and fragrance, the warmth of the fire and the delicious aroma of soup on the stove all threaded together into a blissful feeling that was familiar and yet foreign.

Home. This was what a home felt like. These feelings stirring deep in his psyche were memories of a time long ago, before cancer stole his mother and, by extension, his father, launching his crusade to become an oncologist. For the first time in a long time, he didn't feel a pang of guilt because he wasn't studying or caring for patients. Instead, he felt completely content to just be here with her. *She* made it okay in ways he didn't understand.

But then her hands were gone and the absence of her touch shocked Joe back to reality. The spell was broken—that was if it was ever there in the first place. Lily had hardly asked for some stranger to show up at her front door, let alone hit on her. And he didn't need to get himself mixed up in a relationship when he still had no idea what his future held.

She cast a glance upstairs where he guessed the rest of the bedrooms must be, then back at him. She chewed her lip for a moment, an utterly devastating gesture that tested his resolve to keep his distance.

"Here, let me fix that," she finally said, reaching for his shirt again. Her deft fingers rebuttoned his shirt, affording him one last long gaze at the beauty of her features.

She paused when done, giving him a wan

smile that made him want to ask if everything was okay. But that wasn't his business. She had friends and a daughter. A life of her own in a town that cared about her.

"I'm not finding any breaks, Joe," she said, and he could hear the strain in her voice. "Which is good news. But I think you have a torn rotator cuff. You need an MRI to know for sure, but I do know this. There's no way you'll be able to open the clinic this week."

Joe's chest tightened with resistance. "That's impossible. The clinic hasn't had a doctor for months!"

"The town council will just have to keep relying on temporary health-care workers until you're healed."

Joe broke his gaze with her to frown into the fire. Playing country doc in Twin Creeks had never been part of his life plan. But taking care of people had always been. Maybe his original plan to be an oncologist hadn't worked out like he hoped…yet. But there was no way he could hang out on his couch for weeks while people like Bill ran out of insulin because no one checked on them.

But the deep burning fire in his shoulder told him Lily was right. Whatever that accident had done to him, he was as helpless as a baby.

There was no way he could run the clinic like this. At least, not alone.

He looked away from the fire, his gaze finding Lily.

"You're a nurse," he challenged.

"What?" Her brow knitted in confusion. Then realization bloomed as she read his expression. "Oh, no, Joe. There's no way."

"Why not? You used to be a trauma nurse in Chicago. And you know this town, and the people who live here. Besides, you looked a heck of a lot happier fighting your way through a blizzard to save Daisy than you did when you talked about your journal work."

"That's different."

"Why?" he pressed again.

"Because I'm not a nurse anymore."

"But why not?" He knew he was being intrusive, but it made no sense to close the clinic for another month or two when they both had the skills to keep it open. "What's the deal? Were you injured? In some kind of trouble?"

"Because I can't do that work! Okay?" she shouted, then leaned back against the couch, defeated. Joe tried to make sense of the moment. Clearly, he had touched a nerve in her, but he didn't know why.

"My husband didn't just die, Joe. He was

killed. Connor was a doctor in the emergency department at the hospital where my team and I delivered many of our trauma patients." She fidgeted with a loose thread on her shirt. "He wasn't scheduled to work that night. But we had just found out that I was pregnant with Alexa, and he wanted to start saving to buy our own house as soon as possible."

She folded her arms across her chest, drawing her sweater tighter around her body. "My team was completing a patient handoff when we heard shouting. Someone was approaching the emergency room. A man, very angry, screaming for his wife. We learned later that his wife was a domestic violence victim. He was yelling, demanding to see his wife. Connor wasn't going to allow that. He intercepted the man and tried to get him to calm down. But that only made the man more angry."

She closed her eyes against the memory. "I never saw the gun, but Connor did. All I remember is him yelling *Lily, run!* and then he lunged in front of me."

Joe listened, a heavy knot forming in his chest. Guilt washed over him, realizing how blind he'd been—so consumed with his own need for help at the clinic that he hadn't once stopped to consider why Lily had walked away from nursing. Now, hearing the depth of her pain, her unspoken wounds too raw for him to fully grasp, he felt ashamed, knowing her trauma was far beyond anything he could have imagined or understood.

"I tried to go back to work after Connor died. But something in me broke that night. I thought it would get better with time, but it didn't. I started having anxiety attacks when my team got the call to respond to an emergency. I froze up when I needed to help. I never knew what would trigger me. But I knew there was no room on a medical helicopter for someone who couldn't pull her weight."

Her eyes welled with tears, and she dropped her head to her hands. Instinct more than thought impelled Joe to reach for her hands, pull them away, so he could look into her eyes. "But you *can* do this work. I saw you do it today...for me and Daisy."

"That was different."

"How?"

She shrugged in frustration. "I have no idea, Joe."

"Maybe if we take it slow, like just part-time at first. You take whatever cases you want and leave the rest to me. If I can't help them, we'll arrange medical transport to a facility that can.

I think if we give it enough time, you'll get your sea legs back under you. I think you need this, Lily. And I *know* I need you."

He held his breath, hoping she wouldn't say no. Suddenly, his mission wasn't just to make sure Twin Creeks had a functional medical clinic. It was also to break through the fog of guilt and despair that had convinced this woman she was too broken to ever heal and reclaim the life she wanted.

"I don't know, Joe. I don't want anyone to get hurt."

"Fine. Then let fate decide." He indicated the cards in his hand. "Finish the game. If I win, you work at the clinic. If you win…well, it's up to you what happens next."

"We're going to decide my future based on a round of poker?"

"Why not? Who knows how much of human history has been shaped by wagers, chance and sheer dumb luck. What about the circumstances that led to us even being here right now? What if my mentor had supported my fellowship application in the first place? I never would have come to Twin Creeks and never would have stumbled my way through a blizzard to find you."

"Sometimes fate is awful," Lily whispered.

Sometimes it was. Why did his mom have to inherit the cluster of genes that caused her ovarian cancer? Why did his father lack the strength to go on when she died? And what had fate tucked into his own genetic code?

But the events of the day—saving Grace, then being saved by Lily—were so random and fortuitous, it was hard to ignore the gifts that fate could bring, too.

Lily bit her lip and stared into the fire. "Okay," she finally whispered.

"Okay?"

"Yeah, okay. Let's finish the game. See what happens."

She laid her cards down first, one by one. A two, three, four, five and six…all hearts.

Joe's eyebrow arched as she laid out her cards. He looked down at his hand, his smile melting into a frown. Then he laid his cards out one by one. A five of hearts, followed by a five of spades, diamonds and clubs.

Her straight flush beat his four of a kind. She had won. Her fate was in her hands now.

The fire burned low in the fireplace. A chill crept into the room. The weak afternoon light had surrendered to the dark, so that the light from her lanterns made shadows dance on the wall. Joe braced himself for her answer.

When she spoke, her voice was so soft, he had to strain to hear. "Part of me wants to keep things just as they are. I've worked hard to create a little bubble for me and Alexa, and it's kept us safe for five years now."

He held his breath and willed himself to be still. He wanted to smash the hell out of that little bubble, set her and Alexa free of a life that seemed too small for this vivacious woman. But it wasn't up to him.

"I'm grateful to the bubble. But I hate it, too. Because every day that I try to find my happiness in growing cucumbers and fact-checking articles is one more day that my soul seems to die just a little bit more." She looked away from the fire and to him. Her gaze was different. Something had shifted. He saw it in her clenched jaw, her pointed gaze.

"Okay," she said.

Joe's breath caught. "Okay?"

She stiffened her spine and steeled her gaze. "Part-time, mornings only, while Alexa is in school. And only four days a week. I'll need a day to catch up on journal work."

Was he hearing this right? Was this a yes? "So, you'll do it? Work at the clinic?"

She repeated her terms, slowly and deliberately. "Just until your shoulder is better. Or the town council hires a permanent doctor. No promises, Joe. Okay?"

He nodded slowly, deliberately. "Okay, Lily," he repeated in a soft voice, as if speaking too loudly might make her change her mind. "No promises. For either of us."

Joe used his teeth to tug his glove off, then fished the clinic keys from his jacket pocket with his good arm. It was cold and dark outside, making his breath crystallize into tiny, misty clouds. Starting early on his first day of working at the clinic would give him some time to get his thoughts and the space organized. It also meant he was the only soul in sight on Main Street, where the Twin Creeks Community Clinic sat in an old-fashioned shopping center, tucked between a hardware store and a vacuum repair shop.

His cold, numb fingers nearly fumbled the key. His injured shoulder was still stabilized in a sling, making everyday tasks difficult. But this was a temporary hassle. As soon as the roads were clear after Winter Storm Isabella, he had visited an orthopedic clinic in Billings and gotten good news. The snowmobile accident had badly wrenched his shoulder, but he didn't need surgery. With a few weeks' rest, he should be fully healed and ready to work at full capacity.

He jiggled the key into the door lock and was surprised when the knob turned freely in his hand. The door swung open to reveal a waiting room already full of people. Joe froze and scanned the room. Two elderly women in floral dresses and matching ballerina buns sat shoulder to shoulder on the couch. A lean, pale man in green rubber wading boots sat in the chair beside them, fidgeting with his winter wool hat. A young mother had properly commandeered the only rocking chair in the room and was rocking a small dozing infant. A middle-aged woman who wore her blend of black-and-gray hair in a long braid was the only person not inspecting him from head to toe. She was too busy working furiously at a knitting project that sprawled across her lap.

As surprised as Joe was to find his predawn waiting room already packed with patients, they seemed only curious at his appearance. Time stood still for a moment as everyone except the knitting lady stopped what they were doing to study him.

One of the elderly ladies squinted at him, then leaned close to the other, shouting in her ear. "Look at that, Ruth. He looks just like one of them TV doctors."

The other woman startled, perhaps from a nap. "What?" she shouted.

"Oh, never mind," the first woman groused.

"Um…hello," Joe said, trying to recover. "How did y'all get in the office?"

The knitting woman didn't look up. "With the key, of course."

"And what key would that be?" So far as Joe knew, only he and the mayor had keys to the clinic.

"The key that Dr. Smith kept under the front doormat, of course." *Click-click, click-click.* "Sometimes Dr. Smith went out on house calls, or needed to help if one of his mares was delivering breech. He left a key so folks could let themselves in and be comfortable till he made it back to the clinic."

Joe nodded, trying to take in so much foreign information all at once. "I see. But um, the clinic doesn't usually open until nine, right?"

"That's right." *Click-click, click-click.* "We'll wait."

"All right, then," Joe said. "See you soon, I guess."

There went any plans he had for getting organized before work. It was impossible to focus on anything besides the steady drone of chatter coming from the waiting room.

He might as well get his workday started. Maybe if he started early, he could close a little early, too. This was his first time leaving Daisy alone at home since they had moved to Twin Creeks. He already missed her steady presence by his side.

Joe returned to the waiting room and introduced himself as the new doctor for the community. "At least for a short while as your town council continues to search for a permanent replacement." The knitting woman snorted to herself but didn't look up from her work. He wasn't really sure what that meant, so he refocused on the expectant faces looking his way. "So then, who's first?"

Everyone in the waiting room cast glances at each other with a puzzled expression, as though he had just spoken in a foreign language.

He tried again. "I mean, does anyone have an appointment?"

No one raised their hand or spoke up.

"Okay, who was here first?"

The elderly ladies who looked a lot like sisters just kept beaming big smiles his way. He doubted they heard much of what he said. The young man in the green waders thought that the knitting lady got there before him, but the mother was sure that he had been there first because he'd held her diaper bag while she got the baby out of her car. Soon, they were all talking at once, the din becoming a cacophony of voices until someone shouted, "This isn't how it's done!"

It was the knitting lady again, of course. "Dr. Smith always saw the sickest person first." Her tone held an edge of exasperation, as if this should be perfectly obvious to Joe.

And it did make sense. If you were going to operate a medical clinic without appointments, triaging the walk-ins based on the severity of their illness or injury made sense.

"That's a good idea." *But an appointment system would be better.* "Does anyone have a fever?"

The young mother raised her hand. "My baby woke up feverish this morning and won't nurse."

The knitting woman clucked in sympathy. "He's probably teething, poor thing."

"All right. One fever. Does anyone have a serious injury, shortness of breath, chest pain?"

No one ventured a hand or spoke up. Joe did not like this makeshift system. He was basically asking his patients to triage themselves. That was dangerous because heart attacks could feel like indigestion. A stroke could be confused with a headache. There was too much risk of making a mistake.

He checked his watch. Another hour until the clinic officially opened and Lily would show up for her first shift. He desperately hoped she hadn't changed her mind. He needed someone with her expertise to decide who needed urgent care before the others.

Joe took one last look around the room. Other than the tall man who was a little pale, everyone seemed to be in decent shape.

Joe led the young mother and her baby to the larger of his two exam rooms. Once the blizzard had cleared and the streets of Twin Creeks were drivable again, Joe had spent some time at the clinic getting to know his new workspace. The community clinic was poised at an interesting crossroads between modern conveniences and old-world sentimentality. There were old, faded posters showing various aspects of human anatomy, and glass jars filled with cotton balls and tongue depressors. Peeling linoleum tiles that should have been replaced a decade ago were topped by a surprisingly modern surgical table that could be risen or lowered to Joe's perfect height. It concerned him that Dr. Smith had felt the need to order a surgical table—what kind of cases had the old doctor seen that made that seem like a necessary purchase?

There were also cameras positioned at various points in the room, along with a smattering of microphones built into the walls and added to the surgical table. Joe knew these were a recent investment in the clinic, thanks to the town council. They had signed a contract with a telehealth company that specialized in connecting rural medical clinics with medical specialists all over North America using state-of-the-art, on-demand telehealth equipment. All Joe had to do was press a button on the wall and he was instantly connected with a trained dispatcher who would arrange a virtual consultation with the right specialist for his case.

The baby's ears were clear, but she had plenty of chest and nasal congestion to confirm his suspicions.

"Looks like a run-of-the-mill winter cold," he assured the young mother. "Just give her plenty of fluids and run a humidifier in her room. Maybe some antihistamines for the drainage so she can sleep. She'll be right as rain in a day or two."

He handed baby Mabel back to her mother, who settled the baby on her hip. "So do you have her medication in stock or will you send her prescription to the pharmacy?"

"She doesn't need medication," Joe assured her. "It's just a little virus that will run its course."

"But Dr. Smith always...."

"Mrs. Hawthorne, the protocol for viral rhinitis that is characterized by copious amounts of clear drainage is best treated initially with an antihistamine that has anticholinergic side effects. Now, if it turns out that Mabel has viral-induced rhinitis that is refractory to an antihistamine, I might consider an intranasal ipratropium bromide zero point zero six percent. But at this point, I do not believe Mabel needs that intervention."

The mother's brow furrowed in confusion. "What?"

"It's just a cold, ma'am."

"But she has a fever!"

"Completely normal for viral rhin..." The expression on the mother's face stopped him. "It's normal for a virus. I promise you that Mabel will be just fine."

But instead of looking reassured, Mabel's mom looked angry. "So, you're not going to help my baby?"

"I *am* helping your baby."

"By denying her medicine? When she has a fever?" Mabel began fussing on her hip. "Ugh, you've been no help at all…" She flicked his chest with her finger, right where his name was embroidered in navy blue thread above the breast pocket. *Dr. Chambers.*

As she stomped out of the office, she passed Lily, who was heading in.

"Hey there, Sophia!" Lily said with a big smile. "How's that sweet baby Mabel today?"

"Practically dead, thanks to him!" Sophia indicated Joe with an indignant chin thrust. She headed down the hallway, then paused to turn back and shout, "And I thought a California doctor would have a better tan!"

Lily's mouth gaped as she watched Sophia leave. She turned back to Joe, her eyebrows arched impossibly high. "What did you do?"

"Nothing!"

"Well, I suggest you do *something* next time," she said, her tone full of mirth. She stepped aside to reveal the elderly sisters behind her. "Joe, meet Betty and Ruth, twin sisters who are here for their annual physical. Which exam room would you like to use?"

"I can see them here," Joe said. It was the larger of the two rooms and included the adjustable surgical table along with the telehealth equipment. Not that he expected to need all of that, but the room was much better equipped and comfortable.

Joe was able to tease out their health history in bits and pieces. Betty was the elder sister by two whole minutes. She was talkative and funny but blind as a bat. Ruth, the younger sister, was hearing impaired to the point of deafness, but still able to see well enough to drive their ancient sedan to church and back.

"Between the two of us, we make a whole person!" Betty cackled, and he couldn't help but laugh along.

"So, what brought you in today?" Joe poised his pen over a legal pad. It seemed a terribly unprofessional way to record his patients' visit, but the clinic lacked the tablet computers he was used to using in LA.

They were there for their annual physical. Betty leaned in and asked, in a conspiratorial whisper, if she might get an eye exam done so she could get her driver's license. She cast a sly glance at her sister, who seemed blissfully unaware of the conversation.

"Of course," Joe said, eager to recover from the bad start he had had with Mabel's mother. Betty read the chart perfectly, which was surprising considering her thick eyeglasses, but she didn't hesitate once.

"Practically twenty/twenty," he told her as he signed off on her DMV form.

Just then, he heard Lily shout for help.

"Ladies, could you give me a moment?" He passed the vision form to Betty, who looked like she had just been handed a fabulous prize.

Joe dashed to the waiting room, an uncomfortable surge of adrenaline making his heart rate soar. There had been an unmistakable edge of panic in Lily's voice.

Joe found Lily in the waiting room, crouched in front of the tall, pale man and taking his pulse.

"Joe, why is Luke just sitting here? He's white as a sheet!"

Joe was at a loss for words. "He was fine just a few minutes ago." But was that true? The man had been pale ever since he arrived. But since the man hadn't spoken up when Joe was doing triage, Joe thought that was just the way he looked.

"Sir, what brought you in today?" It was a question he should have asked a long time ago.

The man turned his leg out, revealing a knife handle protruding from the back of his boot. He looked up with an embarrassed grin. "I borrowed my wife's utility knife to scrape some tar off my boot." He shook his head with despair. "She's gonna kill me."

Lily plucked Joe's penlight from his lab coat pocket, then peered into the man's boot. "Would you look at that? You've been quietly bleeding to death in your boot."

Joe rubbed his brow. "You've been stabbed? And you didn't say anything?"

"You asked if anyone had an emergency." He glanced down at his boot. "And this knife wasn't going nowhere."

Joe groaned with frustration. He and Lily helped Luke to the back room for an X-ray.

"Oh, thank God," Lily whispered as she scanned the films.

Joe didn't have to ask what she meant. The knife was short and stubby and had managed to miss Luke's bone. And with the injury in his lower leg, they didn't have to worry about damage to a major artery.

"I'll numb him," Lily said. She went off to prepare a dose of lidocaine while Joe prepared the supplies they would need to remove the utility knife and clean and repair Luke's injury.

Luke watched the entire operation with keen interest. When Joe was done, he turned his leg this way and that, appreciating the vertical line of sutures that ran from midcalf to his ankle.

"That's so cool, Doc. Hope it leaves a Franko scar!" He chuckled and hopped off the table, his gait awkward from walking with one foot in a wading boot and the other barefoot.

Joe watched him leave, shaking his head. "He didn't think it was an emergency…"

Lily was eyeing him from head to toe.

"What?" he said. It was clear she didn't like what she saw. He couldn't imagine why. He was wearing his usual doctor attire. Italian leather loafers, pressed wool pants, a navy blue dress shirt and a gray-and-blue tie to match.

"Nice threads," she said. "Are you the keynote speaker for the—what did you call us?— the Middle-of-Nowhere Medical Conference?"

"Hey," he said. "I already said I was… Wait, what's that sound?"

Lily stopped and listened, her head cocked. "I don't know. But it's coming from your other exam room."

Joe headed that way with Lily close on his heels. He paused to knock before entering but then they both heard an angry whining sound, like someone was standing on a cat's tail. All pleasantries aside, Joe flung the door open and discovered things were not the way he had left them.

The surgical table was the source of the angry whine. The head of the table was tilted as high as it would go, nearly five feet in the air, and the foot side was down almost to the floor. Ruth, the petite half-deaf sister, had slid down the table and landed in a little ball of Queen Anne's lace and sensible shoes. Betty was frantically trying to keep Ruth from falling onto the floor, but Ruth seemed rather oblivious. She just smiled serenely as Betty tugged on her arms.

Joe tried to make sense of the crazy scene. Why was this happening? The table was perfectly fine when he left. Then he looked down and noticed that Betty was standing on the floor pedal that raised and lowered the head of the table. She clearly didn't realize what she was doing, too focused on trying to keep her sister in a semi upright position.

Lily rushed past him. She helped to get Ruth back on her feet, but by now she was so dizzy, she could hardly stand by herself. But the table's motor continued to grind on.

"Your foot," Joe yelled to Betty. She beamed back at him. "You have to move your foot off the pedal!" Joe hollered.

"My foot?" she repeated, confused.

Exasperated, Joe hooked an arm around her waist and lifted her tiny frame off the foot pedal. The grinding, screeching sound came to a merciful end.

"Oh, my," Betty said, smoothing her skirt. "I believe your table may be broken, Doctor."

"Thank you," Joe said through gritted teeth. "I will be sure to look into that."

Lily's mouth was a tight, thin line, but she was having a difficult time suppressing her smile. Somehow, they managed to get through the health concerns of the sisters. Joe wrote a round of prescriptions for both and then they walked them out to the waiting room.

Lily took one last look through their paperwork before they left. "Wait a second—what's this?"

Betty cast her eyes downward.

"Joe, did you sign this form?"

Joe peeked over her shoulder. "Sure. She passed her vision exam with flying colors."

Lily frowned at Betty. "Nice try, Betty." Then she ripped the form in half.

"Damn it," Betty swore under her breath.

For some reason, she took it out on Joe. "Dr. Smith left some pretty big shoes to fill, young man! I'm not sure you're up to the task."

He stood there helplessly. "What happened?"

"Betty's legally blind, Joe. She memorized the vision test years ago."

The sisters left and Joe felt like he could finally exhale. He dropped into a chair opposite Lily's desk as Lily flipped the closed sign for their lunch break.

"Well, let's see," Joe said, using his fingers to tick off his list. "That's two patients who hate me and one I almost killed. Not the most auspicious start."

Lily settled into her chair. "Aw, don't take it too personally. Twin Creeks is a special place, Joe. Folks are going to need a little time to get used to the change."

Special place. Where had he heard that before? Oh, yes, his mentor had told him that when she had exiled him to the American northwest.

Lily zipped open her insulated lunch bag and laid out her lunch. "Trust me, Joe. Folks around here just need a little time to get used to your face. Before you know it, the waiting room will be standing room only."

CHAPTER SIX

JOE RECLINED ON the couch in the clinic's waiting room, bouncing a rubber ball against the wall.

Bounce-bang-bounce. Bounce-bang-bounce.

"How does our morning look, Lily?"

Lily didn't need to open their appointment scheduler to know the answer. "The schedule is wide-open, Joe."

"So, no appointments at all? Not a single patient on the books?"

"Nope."

"And how many people are in the waiting room?"

"Including us? Two."

Bounce-bang-bounce.

"So, just to recap, we have no patients today. Just like yesterday. And the day before. And last week."

Lily rolled her eyes and closed the filing cabinet. It had been like this for over a week, ever since Joe's disastrous first day. Even though Winter Storm Isabella was long gone and the roads were clear and dry, the clinic remained stubbornly empty. Except for one teenage boy who had brought his goat in for an X-ray because the veterinarian's machine was down.

Joe was flummoxed but she had a pretty good idea why the lobby was empty. Joe's first day had been…less than spectacular. There was no doubt in her mind that word had spread all over town at warp speed. So now everyone was avoiding the big-city doc and his big-city ways.

"Look on the bright side," she chided Joe. "With all the downtime, your shoulder should be healed in no time!"

Lily had been thrilled to hear that Joe didn't need surgery. But now she wondered how long she should stick around the clinic. Being alone with Joe had been terrible for her peace of mind. Without a steady stream of patients and problems, she had way too much time on her hands to wonder where he had come from and what his story was. He was friendly enough when it came to clinic business, but otherwise, he kept his nose buried in a book, endlessly preparing for that oncology fellowship he wanted so much. She knew all about that fellowship—it was all he ever wanted to talk about—but he was frustratingly vague about his personal life. Was he being obtuse? Or had he really built his entire life around medicine and oncology?

Eventually, she did what any modern woman would—she checked his social media. Joe didn't post often, but when he did, it was clear he lived by his "work hard, play harder" mantra. His social media was filled with photos of medical school achievements, but just as many showed him enjoying his downtime—ski trips, boating adventures and bonfires on the beach. In every picture, there was a pretty girl on his arm or in his lap, but never the same girl twice.

Honestly, it was a relief to know that he wasn't the committed type. Somehow, over the past few weeks of working together, she had managed to develop the teeniest little…what? *Crush* seemed too strong of a word. *Infatuation* was more like it. And who could blame her? He was handsome and charming and just a little mysterious. It gave her understimulated mind plenty to think about on her long drives back and forth to the clinic. A just-right blend of angst and excitement that added an edge of surprise to a life that was otherwise pretty dull.

But she needed to stop playing these mind

games with herself. Nothing would ever become of her little infatuation. Even if Joe didn't spend every minute of his day plotting his escape from Twin Creeks, there was no way she could let herself fall for him. Losing Connor had broken her into a million tiny pieces, and it had taken her most of the past five years to put herself back together again. There was just no way she could let herself fall for Joe—or anyone, really—and risk having her heart broken like that again.

But it was also a good reason not to spend too long working at the clinic. She wasn't worried about falling head over heels for Joe, but she didn't need to indulge in romantic fantasies that would just leave her feeling lonelier when he left. Still, she'd rather be lonely than head over heels in love with Joe and terrified that any day, he could be snatched away without warning.

Lily checked her watch—an hour till they closed for lunch. She had time to run an errand or two before she needed to pick Alexa up from her morning preschool program.

She closed the file on her desk and pushed away from the counter. "Well, if you don't need anything, I think I'll head out a little early."

Bounce-bang-bounce.

"That's fine."

Lily busied herself finding her purse and winter coat. It was cloudy and cold, and the dim light was making the waiting room look sad and dingy.

She paused at the door, her gloves in hand. "You want the lights on?"

"No need."

Bounce-bang-bounce.

"Okay, then. See you tomorrow."

Maybe it was the low light that made her pause a moment. This wasn't the Joe she had seen on social media, full of confidence and a passion for adventure. This version of Joe looked a little...lost. Maybe he had a revolving door of girlfriends in California, but here in Twin Creeks, he was all alone. And the entire town snubbing him wasn't helping matters at all.

The doorknob felt solid in her hand. Joe's reputation in Twin Creeks wasn't her problem. At least, it didn't have to be. All she had promised was to help at the clinic until his shoulder was healed. In just a few weeks, he would be fine and she could return to her simple, sane life.

Bounce-bang-bounce.

She let out a soft sigh, her gaze drifting downward. It wasn't that simple, and she knew it. After Connor died, she had been all alone in the world. And then Jennifer had offered her a home and friendship in Twin Creeks. Who would do that for Joe?

Joe's head snapped up when she groaned out loud. "You okay?"

Dammit! I hope I don't regret this.

"You like pie, Joe?"

"What?"

"Pie. It's a dessert item with crust and some kind of filling. Sometimes fruit…sometimes custard…"

He rolled to a sitting position. "I know what pie is. And yes, I like it."

Lily silently kissed her uncomplicated life goodbye. "Well, come on, then."

"Where?" But he was already grabbing his coat.

"The Snowy Owl Café. Best pie in town 'cuz it's the *only* pie in town."

Joe closed the door behind them. He started to slip the key into his pocket, but then stopped to look at Lily.

"Don't bother."

"Right," he said before returning the key under the mat.

* * *

Lily parked her truck in front of a quaint log cabin-style building with a snow-dusted roof and twinkling fairy lights strung along the eaves. Joe followed Lily up the wooden steps to the front porch of the café, pausing to check out the intricately carved Snowy Owl that hung over the café's wood door.

"I guess Twin Creeks can be kind of charming," Joe said. "Even if that charm is covered in snow and ice."

Lily laughed and led him into the foyer where they hung up their jackets and hats. A lean woman with silver threaded through her hair recognized Lily and crossed the café to give her a huge hug. "Lily! It's so good to see you."

Lily returned the hug, then introduced the woman as Denise, owner of The Snowy Owl Café.

Denise shook Joe's hand politely. "Pleased to meet you, Dr. Chambers. I've, um—" she suppressed a smile "—heard a lot about you."

Lily smiled, too, in a way that made Joe doubt this was a ringing endorsement of his reputation.

After they ordered, Lily's gaze shifted to

something happening behind him. She chuckled at what she saw.

"What?"

"The Twin Creeks gossip line has been officially activated."

Joe glanced over his shoulder and caught sight of the barista, her gestures lively and animated as she pointed in his direction, her eyes lighting up with whatever story she was telling.

"Don't look now!" Lily hissed.

"Why not?"

"Because they're talking about you!"

"Why would they be talking about me?"

"Because that's what Twin Creeks does, Joe. We eat pie and talk about people."

He studied her face like a detective. "And this is good?"

"It could be. Or it could make things a lot worse. All depends on what they're saying."

"I don't get it."

"Listen, Joe." She leaned in, her eyes locking on to his with an intense gaze. "The only way we're going to start filling the clinic with patients is if Twin Creeks accepts you—both as a resident and as their doctor."

"I don't see how that's going to happen if no one comes to the clinic."

"Exactly. That's why everyone needs to

know who you are," she said. "More importantly, they need to *like* who you are. You could make a difference by fitting in a bit better—maybe ditch the tie and lab coat. Dr. Smith always looked like he came straight from his barn to the clinic. People felt like they were visiting their neighbor, not a scary doctor."

Joe frowned, mulling over her advice. His lab coat was more than just a uniform; it was also a badge of honor, marking his place in the medical hierarchy and reflecting the sacrifices he'd made to earn it. Of course, there was no way she could know that these symbols of status were also his consolation prizes. His early-onset cancer risk meant he would never have a wedding or hear a chubby toddler call him "Daddy." So he clung to trophies like his lab coat, his convertible and off-duty adventures as a source of solace and validation in a world where he would always be alone.

"So that's it? I dress more like a rancher and suddenly I'm the greatest thing since sliced bread?"

She sipped her coffee. "Probably not."

"What else, then?"

Lily set her fork at the edge of her plate and steepled her fingers.

"Folks around here are hardy, prideful people who try not to burden others with their problems. So, if you're going to help them, you have to…you know, show you care about them."

"Well, of course I care about them. Isn't that what doctors do? Take care of people when they're sick or injured?"

"I'm not talking about taking care of their bodies, Joe. I'm talking about caring for *them*."

Joe felt his brow furrow. "I don't get it."

"Take Mabel's mom. She came in with her sick baby, right?"

"Right. But Mabel just had a cold. Once I ruled out allergies and bacterial infection, I correctly recommended plenty of rest and a humidifier to keep her comfortable."

"But her mother wanted medication, right?"

"Right. And I didn't prescribe any antibiotics because Mabel didn't need them."

"What made you think she wanted antibiotics?"

"Because she…" Joe was about to say *asked for antibiotics* but then he realized that wasn't true. She had just asked for medicine.

"Joe, Mabel gets frequent ear infections because she has acid reflux. She's been on an H2 blocker for a few months, which has helped. But sometimes her reflux flares and causes her to develop symptoms of a cold. Dr. Smith prescribed extra acid blockers when she's symptomatic, to try to prevent an ear infection."

Joe frowned. "I took Mabel's medical history before the exam. Her mother didn't mention any of this." Joe felt his patience fraying at this misunderstanding with Mabel's mother. "She should have told me. It's important to consider familial input when choosing a course of action for your patients."

"Mabel's mom didn't want to give you *familial input.* She wanted to tell you how Mabel started crawling last week and how her fine blond hair is finally growing in. Then she wanted to tell you she spent all day making homemade baby food and, oh, by the way, I think her acid reflux might be flaring." Lily cocked her head. "See how that works?"

Joe groaned and leaned back in the booth. "Good grief, Lily. If I have to play this cat-and-mouse game with every patient, appointments will take forever!"

"They'll take exactly as long as they need to take."

Joe considered Lily's suggestions. Sure, he could be a little more social—that wouldn't hurt. Ditching the lab coat and tailored suit?

He didn't really want to do that but whatever. He could make it work.

But trying to forge an emotional connection with every patient? That was way outside his comfort zone. It was why he had chosen medicine as his career. Decisions were made on data and studies, not hunches or feelings.

"Listen, Lily. I *do* care about my patients, but at the end of the day, they are still my *patients*. I have to maintain emotional distance so I can be an effective doctor. After all, when we care *too* much, it can make us want to do the easy thing, instead of the right thing."

Lily opened her mouth to protest, but then Denise reappeared at their table to take their order. She was about to leave when she turned back. "Hey, I guess you two will be taking over the blood drive this year?"

Joe noticed how Lily's shoulders tensed and her gaze faltered. "Oh," Lily said, her voice wavering. "I hadn't thought about that when I agreed to work at the clinic."

Joe's gaze pinged back and forth between Lily and Denise. "Blood drive?"

Denise set down her coffeepot, happy to explain. "Well, Twin Creeks organizes a blood drive twice a year—winter and summer—to make sure that our blood bank is stocked for the year. Dr. Smith was a genius at getting all the tourists to donate. Now that he's gone—" she cast her gaze upward "—I guess it'll be up to you and Lily to run the show."

Lily fiddled nervously with the hem of her sleeve, avoiding Joe's gaze. This was the first time Joe had seen her look so vulnerable, and his concern deepened as he wondered what could be troubling her.

As soon as Denise left, Joe leaned toward Lily. "What's wrong?"

Lily glanced out the window. "Nothing. It's fine. I just hadn't expected that the blood drive might be part of my job."

"You scared of blood or something?"

She rewarded his lame joke with a half smile. "No, I'm fine." But clearly, that wasn't true.

All his resolve to maintain emotional distance vanished in an instant. Lily's distress about this blood drive stirred a deep concern within him, and he needed to understand what was wrong.

He ducked his head so she couldn't avoid his gaze. "Lily, what's up?"

She grabbed a napkin and began twisting it in her hands. "Connor and I planned a winter wedding so we could take our honeymoon in Twin Creeks. We both loved skiing, and Twin Creeks has some of the best skiing in the northwestern US. We were here for the first blood drive and we were two of those tourists Dr. Smith roped into donating blood. We didn't count on it being such a huge community event. The town council provides a huge pancake breakfast and there's all kinds of activities for the kids. What should be a mundane donation event turned out to be so much fun. We just fell in love with Twin Creeks and from then on, we spent every anniversary here."

There was so much emotion in her voice and the story was so sad. Joe almost felt like he was intruding as she shared her story.

"There's a dance, too," she confided, her voice just barely above a whisper. "About a week after the blood drive, the town hosts The Healthy Heart Gala, which is a fancy—or at least fancy for Twin Creeks—charity dance where we raise money for heart disease research."

Sweet mercy, were those tears trembling on her eyelashes? *No, no, Lily, please don't cry.* He wouldn't be able to take that. People cried when they were upset—he had seen plenty of that when he had to deliver difficult news to patients and their families. But that was his cue to escape those hospital rooms, leaving the emotional fallout to those who knew what to do. Like social workers and chaplains.

But sitting here in this little café, with the scent of freshly ground coffee and sweet pie hanging in the air, he was surprised as hell to realize he didn't want to escape Lily and her tears. He wanted to be the reason she didn't cry anymore.

Get a grip, he silently scolded himself.

Lily was a vulnerable widow with a young daughter. The last thing she needed was him complicating her life with signals he had no right to send. He had nothing to offer her— nothing lasting, nothing real. Just the brief time he'd spend in Twin Creeks. And if the universe had any mercy at all, that time would be over soon.

But there had to be *something* he could do to help Lily through this emotional event. Some small action that could make life a little better for her.

"Let me handle the blood drive, Lily. I'm sure I can do that on my own."

Her eyes flickered with hope, and he felt certain she would take him up on his offer. But then her brow furrowed, and she gazed back down at the table. "I can't do that, Joe."

"Why not?"

"Because next to our high school football season, the Healthy Heart blood drive and gala is *the* town event of the year. *Everyone* will be there. Which makes it the perfect time for Twin Creeks to meet their new doctor. And I should be there to help."

He couldn't believe she was willing to put herself into such an emotionally loaded event just for him. There was no reason for it—she barely knew him.

"Okay," he agreed, reaching across the table to clasp her hand. Wanting to give her strength and let her know that she wouldn't be alone.

But what about the gala? The blood drive he could handle. It was predictable and medical and completely in his wheelhouse. But the gala was something else entirely. That was dancing and dresses and elegant flutes of champagne.

Unbidden, an image of Lily in a sexy dress, her body pressed against his as they danced, came to mind. He could practically feel the warmth of her hand in his, see the flecks of gold in her eyes as she gazed up at him. Suddenly, he was flooded with an aching desire that left no doubt in his mind—he had no business taking his colleague to the gala.

He swallowed hard. "But if it's all the same

to you, I'd like to skip the dance. That is, if you agree."

Lily's expression remained pleasant and neutral, but for just a split second, Joe thought he saw a shadow cloud her eyes. It was there and gone so quickly, he wasn't sure if he had imagined it.

She picked up her fork and gave him a brilliant smile. "Oh, no, we don't need to do the dance. Absolutely not!" Then she shifted her attention to her pie, and Joe wondered if he had said something wrong.

"Well, good," he said, clearing his throat and picking his fork back up. "I'm glad we're on the same page!"

What a relief. He had found a way to help Lily through a difficult situation without risking any sticky, confusing emotional stuff. He should feel triumphant, really, at managing all this without losing control of the situation.

Yet, he didn't feel in control at all.

CHAPTER SEVEN

"Forty-eight...forty-nine...fifty!"

Joe rounded the corner just in time to see a young woman in yoga pants and a ponytail finish her last jumping jack before bending over to lean her hands on her thighs to rest. She was panting hard, but she looked pleased. Joe paused, his hands full of supplies, trying to make sense of the scene.

They were in one of the many classrooms at the community center, where he and Lily had arrived before dawn to set up for the blood drive. With assistance from The Healthy Heart Association, they'd transformed a craft room into a passable temporary donation site. Four recliners were set up for donors to relax in during their donation, but only three were occupied—because the fourth donor was busy doing jumping jacks.

Lily was perched on a rolling stool next to

the empty recliner. "Awesome!" she told the young woman. "You ready to get started?"

The young woman had bright blue eyes that seemed to sparkle. She seemed incredibly energetic.

"Almost! Just twenty push-ups to go."

She got right to it, dropping down and bracing her hands on the floor. Joe grabbed a rolling stool and joined Lily.

"What's going on?" he asked under his breath.

"Joe, meet Maggie O'Hara. She owns the fitness studio on Main Street."

"Pleased to meet…oh, you don't have to do that," Joe said.

But somehow Maggie managed to balance herself on one hand so she could shake his hand with the other.

"Maggie's getting ready for her donation," Lily said. As if that explained anything.

Joe's eyebrow arched. "With push-ups?"

"Helps with blood flow!" Maggie panted.

"That's very conscientious, Maggie, but you don't really need to do that. The Healthy Heart Association just recommends that you have a light meal and hydrate well before…"

Joe trailed off as he caught the look that Lily gave him. He was doing it again—focusing on rules and protocols instead of what his patient might need. He gave Lily a baleful smile.

"But you know, I'm sure a few push-ups won't hurt."

"Twenty!" Maggie huffed. Somehow she bounced catlike from a prone position on the floor back to her feet, brushing her hands off when she landed. "So, you're the new fancy doc I've been hearing about."

It was more of a statement than a question.

"Fancy? No. But yeah, I'm Dr. Joe Chambers."

Maggie gave him the once-over. "You work out much, Dr. Chambers?"

"Sure, when I have time."

"You should stop by the studio. I think you'd love my six-week Build-a-Booty Boot Camp series. Good for flat butts."

Joe fought off the urge to look at his backside. "Thanks for the tip, Maggie. I just might do that. So, you think you're ready to donate?"

Maggie paused and put two fingers on her wrist, checking her pulse. "I think so."

Lily started snapping on a pair of latex gloves while Maggie settled in the chair. Joe picked up his box of supplies, preparing to restock before he helped the next donor.

"Thanks for being patient, you guys. I just

wanted to make sure I didn't get any heart flutters during the donation."

Joe froze and turned back, his gaze immediately meeting Lily's. She looked concerned but kept her gaze steady and calm.

"Flutters?" Lily asked. Her tone was light, but Joe could hear the undercurrent of worry.

Maggie waved her off casually. "It's nothing, really. Only happens when I go for a run."

Joe felt a surge of alarm. He couldn't let this slide. He began firing off a series of medical questions about the flutters, but the more he pressed, the more anxious Maggie became, her earlier ease disappearing.

Lily shot Joe a warning look—a reminder of what she'd tried to tell him back at The Snowy Owl. Patients weren't just their symptoms; they were people, with lives and fears that couldn't be reduced to medical charts.

Realizing he needed a softer approach, Joe shifted tactics. Maggie was passionate about fitness—maybe he could use that to get her to the clinic. "You know," he began, his tone more casual, "we could use some help designing fitness programs for patients recovering from surgery or illness. Do you think you could come by the clinic and talk about the classes you teach?"

Maggie lit up, thrilled at the idea of helping Twin Creeks stay fit. "I'd love that!"

After she left, Lily turned to him with a playful grin. "Not bad, Doc. But you know she's never going to agree to testing unless you take that booty class, right?"

Joe groaned, realizing she was probably right.

Lily shrugged. "Think of it as your Twin Creeks souvenir."

"Does it come with a T-shirt that says *I went to Twin Creeks and all I got was this lousy booty*?"

"More like *Welcome to Twin Creeks. You Must Be Lost*."

"Now that's a T-shirt I would buy!"

Lily shook her head with an amused smile. "I don't know, Doc. I still think Twin Creeks is gonna grow on you."

The rest of the afternoon passed with few complications, as a steady stream of donors came and went, many of them curious about the new doctor they'd heard so much about. Joe and Lily crossed paths repeatedly, her quiet encouragement keeping him grounded as the endless small talk frayed his nerves. Lily seemed to know nearly everyone in Twin Creeks, and the townspeople were thrilled to see her at an event she had avoided for so long. Though she remained poised and gracious all day, Joe noticed the shadows behind her smiles—the way her lips would fall into a soft frown when she thought no one was watching.

Joe tried to stay focused on his tasks, but Lily's quiet struggles gnawed at him. She barely knew him, yet he couldn't shake the urge to ease the sadness that seemed to cling to her all day.

When a lull came in the donor line, he saw his chance.

"Hey, I'm gonna step out for a minute, if that's okay."

"Sure." She looked up from the computer where she was updating their records, giving him a soft smile that made him forget, just for a moment, the exhaustion of the day.

Joe headed to the recreation room, guided by the rich aroma of coffee, bacon and sweet treats. He filled a large mug with strong coffee and doctored it just the way she did at the clinic—two creams and one sugar. When he returned, Lily was alone at the sign-in desk, her attention on the paperwork. Quietly, he placed the coffee next to her elbow.

"What's this for?" she asked, glancing up.

"Just something to make your day a little better."

Her wry smile faded into a slight frown. "It's that obvious, huh?"

"Not really. You're doing great."

"I thought I was holding it together pretty well. But I can't deny that being here stirs up a lot of memories for me."

Joe paused, then spoke softly. "I once over-heard a hospital social worker tell a patient that grief is just all the love we didn't get to give. So maybe feeling sad is just…another way of loving."

She looked at him, her eyes softening. "I like that, Joe." Her smile grew warmer. "I'm so glad you're here."

Before he knew what was happening, she stepped into his arms, surprising him. Instinctively, he wrapped her in his embrace, felt her head rest against his chest. A rush of emotion flooded through him—feelings he'd long since buried now unleashed by the simple, undeniable comfort of having her tucked against his body. The way she smelled, the way she fit so perfectly in his arms, was undoing him piece by piece.

Then she stepped away and it took every ounce of control he had to stuff those emotions back into their box. She gave him a look that was just a beat longer than it needed to be. Nothing dramatic or obvious. But enough to make him wonder if she was catching feelings, too.

Don't look at me like that, Lily. I'm not the guy. Trust me.

Joe took a step back, needing to put some distance between them, forcing himself to get his head on straight. He quickly rearranged his features into the neutral expression he'd perfected over the years. He wasn't always as in control of his emotions as he wanted to be, but he had mastered the art of making it look like he was.

But Lily was different. Her face was an open book, her heart's truths playing out for the world to see. She was honest and vulnerable in a way he couldn't afford to be. She didn't live her life with an invisible clock ticking down her fate. And if she knew he did, she wouldn't be looking at him like that.

"Well, we'd better get back to work, right?" he said, his voice thick with words unsaid.

Lily held his gaze for a few more seconds, searching for something he knew he could never give. Her expression faltered slightly, but she quickly recovered and turned back to the task at hand.

Joe threw himself into the work, grateful for the distraction. The final wave of donors kept them both busy, and the familiar routine of boxing up supplies to return to the Healthy Heart Association helped him push his emotions aside.

But just when he thought he had regained control, he turned from stacking the totes to find Lily bent over the last one, snapping it shut. The brief, unintentional brush of her body against his—her backside grazing his thigh— sent a jolt through him. The suppressed desire he'd been holding back all day surged like a storm inside him, a force powerful enough to wreck both of their lives.

Lily spun around, and in an instant he knew his mask had fallen. She could see everything he was trying so hard to hide.

Their eyes met, and the air between them seemed to thicken as he felt a magnetic pull drawing them closer despite the unspoken barriers. Lily's soft gaze lingered, her lips parting slightly as if she was about to say something but couldn't find the words. Joe felt a dangerous awareness settling in his chest. He could see it in her, too—the way her breath hitched, her cheeks flushing with the same tension that gripped him. But her vulnerability shimmered just beneath the surface, forcing Joe to step back. He couldn't—wouldn't—cross that line. Not with her, not when she deserved so much more than the heartbreak he knew he'd bring.

"Mommy!"

Alexa's sudden cry startled Lily, making her jump as she spun to face her daughter. Alexa raced across the room, her hands overflowing with the artwork she had created during the children's activities. Joe watched as Lily showered her with delighted praise, admiring each piece like a treasure.

The tension in Joe's chest slowly eased, his emotions settling. He was grateful for Alexa's interruption—it was a much-needed reminder of the boundaries he needed to maintain. The day's events had made that crystal clear. He had only wanted to support Lily through a tough event, but the depth of his attraction had blindsided him. From now on, things had to stay strictly professional.

"Mommy, what are you going to wear to the dance?" Alexa asked, her eyes wide with curiosity.

Lily smiled, gently smoothing her daughter's hair. "My pajamas, sweetheart. Because I'm staying home with you."

Alexa frowned. "But you have Dr. Joe now! You could go to the dance with him!"

Joe's pulse spiked as alarm bells rattled his core. Taking Lily to the gala was the *last* thing he needed. More space from Lily was what he needed to keep his head straight. But Alexa was looking up at him with those big, hopeful eyes. What could he possibly say to this adorable little girl? *No, I won't take your mom to the dance?* What would his next trick be— kicking puppies?

Of course, he could take Lily to the gala. He'd spent a lifetime giving beautiful women the night of their lives. He knew how to plan the perfect evening, full of romance and glamour, because that was *all* he had to give. A few dates, a little charm, nothing deeper.

He could do this for Lily, too. It felt right, in a way—giving her a night to remember at an event clouded by painful memories. He just had to keep his heart out of it. And make sure she did, too.

Lily gripped the steering wheel of her truck tightly as she navigated the familiar streets of Twin Creeks. Her heart was already pounding in anticipation of what lay ahead. She glanced over at Joe in the passenger seat. He was still talking to Denise on his cell phone, getting as many details as he could before they arrived on the scene of the accident.

It had been years since she had responded to a trauma call. Her old lettuce-hauler of a truck was a far cry from the state-of-the-art medical helicopter that used to whisk her between accidents and emergency rooms. She tried to stay focused on the road ahead of her, but she still felt haunted by memories of how her skills had failed her after Connor's death. Her hands felt clammy, and her breath came in short, shallow gasps as she tried to focus on the road.

The call for help had come in while she and Joe were working at the clinic. It was a week after the blood drive event and Joe and Lily had settled back into their clinic routine. Lily had recognized Denise's voice, the owner of the Snowy Owl Café, but she could barely understand what Denise was saying.

He won't open his eyes, Lily. I can't get him to open his damn eyes!

Denise had called emergency services, but there was no way of telling how long it would take for them to respond. So Joe and Lily had closed the clinic and were now speeding through Twin Creeks on their way to the quiet neighborhood where Denise and her husband, Matt, lived.

"We're almost there," Joe said, his voice calm and steady. He reached over and gave Lily a reassuring squeeze on the shoulder with his good arm. "Whatever happens next, Lily, remember that we're a team, okay? We'll handle this together."

Lily gave him a wan smile and tried to draw strength from his words. But they both knew the truth. Joe's shoulder injury meant that if there was any intensive hands-on work to do, it would fall to her. She wouldn't be able to sit on the sidelines this time and let her crew take over. Matt's life was literally in her hands.

Oh, please, let emergency services get there before we do.

They pulled up to a modest suburban home where Denise was waiting. She led them quickly to the backyard where Matt lay motionless. Denise frantically ran to his side to kneel beside him.

"Please, you have to help him!" Denise cried as they approached. Her eyes were wide with fear, and her hands shook as she reached for Matt's limp hand.

Joe knelt down, tunneling his focus on Matt.

"Denise, I need you to step aside. We have to assess Matt's injuries."

Matt lay flat on his back, blood pooling around his head. A tall ladder was tipped over the border hedges to land in the snow. A rectangular chunk of ice in the snow told the story. Matt had been trying to clear an ice dam from his roof gutter when he fell.

Denise whimpered with fear and reluctantly let go of Matt's hand. Joe tugged his stethoscope from around his neck. "Lily, we need to assess his airway. Can you take a look?"

Lily's heart started hammering in her chest at the sight of all that blood around Matt's head. She felt that familiar cold dread creep up her legs to her torso and chest, as if her fear lived in the ground, just waiting to invade her in times of stress.

Move, Lily. Just get to Matt's side. You'll know what to do when you get there.

But her legs were like twin blocks of stone, refusing to move again. Her throat tightened with fear. This wasn't like the Shop-n-Go. Joe was injured now, and emergency services were nowhere to be found. If she wasn't able to help Matt, he might die. Her vision blurred for a moment, images of Connor's violent death flashing before her eyes.

"Lily!" Joe's voice was firm, commanding her attention. "You are the best person to help Matt right now. Just trust yourself. Like I do."

Lily gasped. *Trust.* Was that the missing piece of her life? Trust that the world was a safe place to raise her child. And trust that she still had the skills and mental toughness needed to work under crisis.

It was true. She hadn't believed in herself for a very long time. But Joe did. He *trusted* her. More importantly, he needed her.

"Okay." Lily swallowed hard and she walked stiff-legged to Matt's side. She dropped to her knees so hard, she knew she'd have angry purple bruises on her kneecaps the next morning. Her hands were unsteady as she checked Matt's airway.

She looked up to find Joe's steady gaze. "He's not breathing," she told him.

Joe swore under his breath. "And his pulse is weak and erratic." He reached up to cup his injured shoulder with his hand. "Lily, I don't trust my shoulder for something this important. You're gonna have to intubate him."

Joe had stopped wearing his sling to work, but he was not yet fully healed. Lily knew he was right—his weak shoulder was a huge risk right now.

A wave of nausea washed over Lily. Intubations were tricky and complex even for experienced medical professionals. Other than ongoing training to keep her nurse practitioner license current, she had barely touched a real patient for the past five years. Intubating a real patient with head trauma was nothing like working on a mannequin. She knew what she needed to do, but her panic was rising again, threatening to overwhelm her.

Joe's calm voice cut through the haze. "Lily, listen. I'm right here with you. You won't be alone. Just remember your training."

Lily's hands trembled as she took the intubation kit from Joe. Her chest felt so tight, she feared Joe might have to resuscitate her when this was over. Joe moved closer, leaning his hip against hers so that his body became her steady anchor.

"Lily, look at me," Joe said, his voice like a lighthouse beacon through the storm of her panic and fear. "Take a deep breath. In and out."

She did as he asked, even though her breaths were shallow and ragged.

"Now focus on Matt. You know what to do."

Lily forced one more choppy breath, keeping her gaze focused on Joe's deep blue eyes. She found no panic or doubt there. Just his unwavering confidence and calm demeanor. Slowly, her breath steadied, and she felt a small measure of control return.

"That's it," Joe soothed. "Now, let's do this. Together."

Lily nodded, feeling something inside her sharpen and focus. She smeared a thin layer of lubricant on the endotracheal tube, then guided it into Matt's airway. She held her breath as she connected the ambu bag, then began to ventilate him, her hands steadying as she fell into the familiar rhythm of the procedure.

Joe pressed his stethoscope to Matt's chest. "We've got breath sounds. You did it, Lily."

A tsunami of relief washed over Lily's entire body. Denise watched from a distance, her hands pressed to her mouth. "Is he going to be okay?"

Joe looked up at her, his expression just as calm and reassuring as he had been with Lily. "We're doing everything we can, Denise. Emergency transport should be here soon. But until then, he's in good hands with us."

With us.

His words lodged in Lily's heart, knowing that it was their teamwork that had made the difference. Joe had not only found a way to snatch Matt from death's cold, sharp claws, he had also managed to break through the brick wall of fear and doubt that had paralyzed her for so long.

Minutes felt like hours as they kept Matt stable and waited for help. Finally, she heard the distinctive *whomp-whomp-whomp* of an approaching helicopter. A few minutes later, a nurse and EMT in flight suits rushed into Denise's backyard.

"What have we got?" the nurse asked Joe.

Joe didn't answer, instead indicating they should get the patient handoff from Lily.

She cleared her throat. "We have a male patient, age forty-five, found unconscious after falling off a ladder. Patient was not breathing and had a weak, erratic pulse. Intubation was performed on scene using a seven point five millimeter endotracheal tube to secure the airway. No medications given. Recommend continued mechanical ventilation and immediate transport to a level three trauma center."

The trauma nurse nodded. "Good work getting him stabilized. We'll take it from here." She and the EMT prepared Matt for transport, then ran with his stretcher back to the helicopter. Lily followed, with Joe and Denise close behind.

"Where are they taking him? Can I go with him?" Denise couldn't contain her tears anymore. They spilled down her cheeks. Lily instinctively wrapped her arms around her friend as tight as she could, wanting to shield her from everything bad that could happen. She and Joe had managed to stabilize Matt, but he had a long way to go.

The pilot started the helicopter, and Lily's pulse thrilled at the distinctive whirring of the helicopter's rotor blades as it prepared for take-off. There was a rush of wind as the downwash from the rotor blades intensified. Ice and snow swirled about, adding to the dynamic atmosphere.

Lily caught a brief glimpse of the flight nurse's profile as she worked on Matt. For the next twenty minutes, it would be her sole responsibility to keep Matt stable until he reached the emergency room. Lily bit her lip as she watched the nurse work. That was her once, not that long ago. For the first time in five years, she wondered if one day, that might be her again.

The sounds of the engine and rotor blades grew more distant, gradually fading away as the helicopter disappeared from view.

Joe and Lily helped Denise arrange a ride

to the hospital with a neighbor. When Denise was on her way, Joe walked Lily back to her truck where Daisy was waiting patiently. The sun dipped low in the sky, making the cold day even more bleak.

Lily was happy to hand her truck keys over after the emotional afternoon. Joe fired up the truck and looked her way. "I don't know about you, but I'm famished. Wanna grab something to eat?"

"I would love to," Lily said, settling her weary body against the truck seat. "But I've got to get back to Alexa. I don't want to abuse Jennifer's free babysitting offer." She also just wanted to see Alexa and smell that sweet-little-girl scent that pooled in the hollow of her throat. Days like these were terrible reminders to keep her loved ones close, because every day brought its own surprises.

"Why don't we bring dinner back to your place?" Joe suggested, casting a sideways glance at her.

Lily hesitated, her mind swirling with uncertainty. For days, she had wanted to talk to Joe about the upcoming gala. It was clear he didn't really want to go—he'd made that obvious back at The Snowy Owl. He had only agreed because Alexa had put him on the spot.

But the clinic had been bustling ever since the blood drive. Joe's charm and warmth with the donors had endeared him to the town, and now their waiting room really was standing room only.

Joe waited for her response, looking effortlessly handsome. Exhaustion from the stress of saving Matt after his fall weighed heavily on her, and she was ravenous. It just didn't seem like the right time to tell him she was canceling their plans.

So yes, she would invite him back to her house. They could have dinner with Alexa, and once she was in bed, Lily would let him off the hook for the dance. It was only right.

Still, when Joe gave her that smile that made her toes curl in her boots, she couldn't help but wonder why doing the right thing sometimes felt so lousy.

CHAPTER EIGHT

LILY WATCHED WITH a smile as Joe and Alexa huddled over the board game spread out on the living room floor. Joe was dramatically pretending to cheat, slipping extra cards into his hand with exaggerated stealth, just so Alexa could catch him and scold him indignantly. Daisy sat between them, her gaze ping-ponging back and forth as the drama played out. She seemed just as amused by the game as they were. Lily cupped her coffee mug with both hands and felt her heart swell with joy as she watched her daughter have the time of her life.

Joe, with his easy charm, had embraced the role of playful accomplice effortlessly. Lily had to give him credit—he hadn't even flinched when Alexa roped him into taking her mom to the gala. It was sweet of him to play along, but Lily planned to let him off the hook as soon as they were alone.

"Come on, Alexa—time for bed, sweetie," Lily said gently.

Alexa groaned and protested, dragging her feet, but Lily managed to get her settled into her room. After reading her favorite story twice, Lily closed the door softly and headed downstairs.

When Lily walked into the living room, she was taken aback. Joe had transformed the space into a cozy retreat. He'd cleared her coffee table and draped one of her gauzy scarves over it, setting out two glasses of wine that glowed a rich ruby in the firelight. Soft instrumental folk music played from the Bluetooth speaker—a tune that wasn't on her playlist, suggesting Joe had connected his phone to her speaker.

She settled onto the couch, taking a glass of wine, her nerves barely contained.

"Any more news on Matt?" she asked.

"He has a skull fracture with some bleeding in the brain. He's in the ICU while the neuro team figures things out."

"That's terrible. Poor Denise," Lily said, her heart aching for her friend.

Joe sat down beside her, his warmth making her shift closer. "I went to med school with one of the neurologists treating Matt. He's a good guy. He says the neuro team is top-notch."

That was reassuring, though Lily couldn't shake her nervousness. Joe's smile was warm and genuine, but it set a flutter of butterflies loose in her stomach. She looked away, trying to steady herself.

Could she ever have a cozy domestic scene like this? It was the first time she'd thought about it since her disastrous attempts at dating. Yet, she realized she didn't want to open her heart to just any man—only Joe. What was it about him that made her want to push past her boundaries and hope for more?

"You don't have to take me to the gala this weekend," she said, trying to keep her voice steady. "It was very kind of you to offer, but you really don't have to."

"But what if I want to?" His response was quick and firm, leaving her momentarily speechless.

What was his story? Why was he spending time with her and Alexa? Joe was a drop-dead gorgeous doctor, and Lily had noticed the parade of young singles dropping by the clinic with vague complaints. In a small town like Twin Creeks, a handsome single doctor was bound to attract attention. So why was he here, in her living room, spending the night playing little kid games and hanging out with her?

"Well, I'd say that would be…weird," she said.

He laughed. "Why would that be weird?"

"I don't know…" She didn't want to tell him the truth. That she spent most Saturday nights on the couch with a good book and an oversize bowl of popcorn. "I didn't think you'd be into small-town traditions like the gala."

Joe shrugged, his arm casually draped over the back of the couch. "Who knows? Maybe this middle-of-nowhere town is growing on me." He smiled as he threw her words back at her, his fingers grazing her shoulder.

Lily laughed, feeling the warmth of his touch and the sincerity in his eyes. For the first time in a long while, she let herself entertain the possibility of more.

"How did you end up here, Joe? I know you mentioned your mentor sent you, but I don't really know why. Did you lose a bet? Owe someone money back in LA?" She laughed at how she had recycled Joe's joke, then tilted her head, admiring his handsome profile.

Joe rolled his head to face her as they lounged on the couch, his smile tinged with something more somber. "Not quite that sordid. My mentor has known me for a long time. For the past eight years, I've been focused on a career in oncology. But I guess she thought I'd become too fixated on my goals."

He paused, his gaze distant. "My mom died of cancer in her forties. My dad was devastated and turned to drinking. I was just a kid when my mom passed—helpless to support her or my family. I chose oncology as a way to fight back against a disease that caused so much suffering for my family and so many others."

Lily's heart softened. His intense focus on his oncology fellowship suddenly made sense. It wasn't about status or prestige, as she'd first thought. He was driven by a desire to create something positive out of his own profound loss.

She considered his words, reflecting on the power of his commitment. "What a powerful way to show the world all the love you didn't get to give, Joe."

He returned her smile, and as his warm hand rested on hers, a shiver of electricity ran through her. It brought her back to their moment at the blood drive, when she had brushed against him while packing up supplies. In that fleeting instant, she had seen a spark of passion in his eyes that mirrored her own feelings.

But as quickly as it had appeared, it vanished, leaving Joe's expression once again as unreadable as ever.

"Oh, crap. Tell me my watch is broken," Joe groaned, tapping his watch face.

Lily glanced at the clock on the mantel. "That can't be right."

"It is, I'm afraid. I'd better head out," Joe said, getting up from the couch. Lily felt a pang of loss as his warmth left her side.

She followed him to the hallway, where he shrugged into his coat and scarf. The tension in her body was palpable as their flirtation was coming to an abrupt end. It left her feeling restless and unsatisfied.

As he opened the back door, the cold air rushed in. Lily followed him out, wanting to make sure the exterior lights were on so he could see his way back to his car.

"Thanks for dinner," he said, leaning in to kiss her cheek.

But she turned back from the light switch just then, and his kiss landed on her lips.

She registered the warm, light pressure of his mouth. Could feel his breath drift across her skin and scent hints of plum from the wine they had shared.

Both shocked, they broke off the stolen kiss

to stare at each other. Neither moved and the space between them seemed to crackle with energy. She scanned every inch of his face, lingering on the fullness of his lips and the tiny endearing mole that sat just above the curve of his smile. Her eyes traced the line of his jaw, the slope of his cheek, until she found him staring down at her with those hypnotic blue eyes.

Dammit. I hope I don't regret this.

A sense of certainty she had not felt in years warmed her body and strengthened her resolve. She laced one hand around the nape of his neck to draw him in, but he was already moving toward her, his eyes hazy with lust.

She stood on tiptoe, her lips brushing against his with a tantalizingly soft touch. The heat from his mouth surged through her, igniting a fire deep within her core. As his hands curved around her waist, pulling her closer, their kiss grew more intense. Their tongues met in a dance of longing, and she felt as if an invisible weight had been lifted, setting her heart free.

She clung to his jacket, her grip tight with a desperate need she hadn't felt in years. The kiss was all-consuming, a hungry reunion after a five-year hibernation of solitude and unfulfilled desire. She never wanted it to end, but as time passed, their lips finally parted. She glanced at her hands still clutching his coat and wondered with breathless anticipation—if this kiss was so electrifying, what would it be like to make love to him?

With the greatest of willpower, she pushed herself away from Joe's embrace. She kept her eyes averted, hoping he couldn't read her stormy emotions. There was nowhere to go with this attraction. Twin Creeks was not where Joe wanted to be. And she had no idea if her heart could handle what promised to be a short, incredibly passionate fling.

"I've got to get back to Alexa," she said. She had to do the right thing for her daughter. If Alexa woke in the morning to find Joe and Daisy there, her happiness would shoot her to the moon and back. She would never want to let that feeling go. And she wouldn't understand when it was time for Joe to leave in a few months.

The night was getting too cold and her toes were going numb, so they parted for the last time. He waved as he rounded her driveway. She stood in the doorway, hugging herself hard, and watched until his taillights disappeared into the cold, dark night.

But the struggle within her wasn't over. Something fierce in her wanted to call him back, to seize the fleeting chance they had. Joe wouldn't stay in Twin Creeks forever—she knew that well enough. Yet, he was here now, and she couldn't help yearning for something just for herself. A primal and restless need that would awaken her soul from its long slumber and make her feel alive again. The thought of calling him back was almost intoxicating. But she hesitated, knowing that saying yes now would only lead to a heart-wrenching good-bye later. A goodbye she wasn't sure her heart could bear.

CHAPTER NINE

JOE SET THE parking brake and turned off his car's ignition. Lily's small cabin sat nestled in a blanket of pristine snow with a tidy stack of firewood neatly arranged by the door. Even though it was winter, Lily's love for gardening was evident in the carefully pruned bushes and the dormant flower beds lining the path to her front door. Something about her cabin always beckoned to him, inviting him to please come in, have some coffee, stay awhile. Or maybe it was just Lily who made him feel like that.

Joe glanced at the passenger seat, where a stunning bouquet of roses and an expensive bottle of champagne awaited. These luxuries were rare in Twin Creeks, so he had made the long drive to Billings on a Saturday afternoon while Lily was occupied with Alexa. He'd also treated himself to a fresh haircut and picked out a new shirt and tie. To top it off, he'd had his car meticulously detailed, ensuring the midnight-black exterior gleamed and the rich, buttery leather seats smelled fresh and a little soapy.

Joe checked his reflection in the rearview mirror and made a few last-minute adjustments. He didn't understand the undercurrent of nervousness that had been dogging him all day. He had crafted the evening with fastidious care, determined to give Lily the night of her life. Usually, he looked forward to dates with eager anticipation, knowing he could pour himself into the role of charming bachelor date for the night because there would be no second date.

But tonight felt different. Probably because of that passionate kiss. Ever since he had tasted Lily's lips, she had haunted his thoughts with an intensity he hadn't anticipated. Memories of how she had pulled him closer and the fierce passion in her kiss had left him feeling completely disoriented. Something about that kiss had shaken him in a way that said Lily was different. It had left him feeling vulnerable and, for once, unsure of his own usually unshakeable demeanor.

So he had done his best to keep his distance at the clinic, trying to get his emotions back under control. It was pure agony to hear her voice in the hallway or catch sight of her between patients and know that he needed to stay away. But Lily seemed to avoid him, too, so he had to conclude that she also felt uneasy with that unexpected kiss. Maybe she even regretted it. He did not, but he was wise enough to know that allowing this attraction to grow would only end badly for both of them.

Despite the nervous flutter beneath the polished image he had cultivated for the evening, he was determined not to let it show. He could manage this—he had spent a lifetime perfecting the art of compartmentalizing his desires from his duties. Tonight Lily deserved an attentive and supportive companion, someone who could help her navigate an event that might stir up painful memories. He was ready to be that person for her.

That realization shook him to the core. Somehow Lily had slipped past the wall he had erected between himself and the world. He was no longer satisfied playing the role of perfect romantic suitor for the night. He wanted more—not for himself but for Lily. He needed her to feel safe and protected, so her heart could finally heal and she could reclaim her life. Letting his guard down—letting these hopes see the light of day—left him feeling bewildered and confused. But he had never felt so acutely alive in his entire life.

Jennifer answered the door, her eyebrows lifting in approval at the sight of Joe's bouquet and champagne. She was watching Alexa while Lily finished getting ready for their date. While he waited, Joe entertained Alexa with amusing tales of what Daisy had been like when she was a mischievous puppy. The more time he spent in Lily's home, the more confident he felt about handling the evening. He just needed to channel the old Joe—charming, self-assured and perfectly in control.

"Hey."

He had been so absorbed in deciphering Alexa's still babyish dialect that he hadn't noticed Lily coming downstairs. But the look on Jennifer's face made him suspect that tonight might not be the surefire success he had anticipated.

He turned to find her on the stairs and in that moment, he knew he was in deep trouble. Because Lily was nothing short of sheer perfection.

She was gorgeous in a strapless black dress that showed off the curve of her shoulder and the delicate skin of her collarbone. A deep slit on the side of the dress revealed her long, shapely legs. She must have gone shopping, too, because the warm, airy blend of spices and fresh florals in her perfume was not familiar and it set his head swimming. It made him think of warm, faraway places he would like to take her to where they could finally be alone.

Joe's heart beat harder as his mouth went dry. All of his senses went on full alert. She was a beautiful woman on any day of the week, but tonight she left him speechless.

"Hey, yourself," he managed to say. "You look beautiful." Which sounded so stupid. Because saying Lily was beautiful was like saying the sun was warm—obvious, undeniable and utterly inadequate to capture the way she lit up everything around her.

She flashed him a dazzling smile that sent Joe's emotions into a dizzying spin. So much for being the epitome of stoicism and control. All he could hope for now was to keep these tumultuous feelings well hidden.

Lily kissed Alexa for the night and thanked Jennifer for babysitting again.

"It's my pleasure, sweetie," Jennifer said, giving Lily a warm smile. "In fact, if it's okay with you, I'd like to keep Alexa at my place. She can stay up a teensy bit past her bedtime and camp out on the couch if she likes."

"Sure," Lily said with a shrug. "If you're sure you don't mind."

Joe carefully navigated the dark forest roads that led back to the highway that would take them to Twin Creeks's downtown. He kept both hands curved around the steering wheel and his eyes on the road, trying hard to keep his thoughts where they belonged. But he couldn't stop stealing glances at her profile. Her black hair was soft and glossy, and her lips were full and red. He wasn't used to this version of Lily, and it was scrambling his thoughts.

Lily glanced at him with a teasing smile. "I can't believe you're wearing a tux, Joe. You clean up pretty well."

Joe grinned but kept his tone light. "Me? What about you? Not bad for a lettuce farmer—not bad at all."

Lily covered her mouth with her hand, embarrassed and amused at the same time. "Oh, my gosh, I remember that morning. I was so worried I had chicken feathers stuck in my hair!" She shyly glanced his way. "You look really nice, Joe."

Joe kept his eyes on the road, not wanting her to see how her compliment affected him. "Nice? That's it? I was going for devastatingly handsome."

Lily rolled her eyes but her smile lingered. "Well, I didn't want to inflate your ego *too* much before we even got there."

Joe couldn't stop himself. "You look stunning, by the way."

She looked down at herself and smoothed her dress with her hands. "Thanks," she said shyly. "Jennifer made me go shopping."

They fell into a brief silence, the air crackling with unspoken tension. Lily's gaze wandered out the window as she nervously toyed with the pendant on her necklace, and Joe couldn't help but wonder if she, too, felt the simmering attraction beneath their playful banter. The anticipation of this night had been a constant thrill for him all week. She crossed her legs, making the fabric of her dress slip to reveal the soft, inviting skin of her thigh. He felt an irresistible urge to reach across the car's cabin so his pinky finger could graze the delicate skin of her knee and feel the warmth of her touch.

By the time they reached the community center, Joe's head was spinning with desire. He was happy to get out of the car and deeply inhale Montana's cold, brisk winter air. It revived him a bit and brought him back to his senses. Even though Lily was a gorgeous, desirable woman, he was not going to make a move on her. She deserved better than the one-and-done dates he had to offer, and there was no way he could step into the unknown and risk sharing his uncertain future with her.

Thankfully, the evening started as a whirlwind of meeting and greeting Twin Creeks's many residents and friends. Lily had been right. Working the blood drive together had been the perfect icebreaker to introduce Joe to the community. Now his night was filled with hearty handshakes and polite inquiries as to where he came from and how he found his way to Twin Creeks.

People were thrilled to see Lily attending the gala for the first time in years. She accepted all of their hugs and well wishes with grace. Joe watched closely for any signs of the sadness that he had seen at the blood drive. But she seemed relaxed and happy to be there.

"I can't believe how much people have changed," she commented thoughtfully. "Rebecca Morales just asked me to write a recommendation letter for her application to medical school. When I first moved here, she had just gotten her first job at The Snowy Owl!" She took a sip of her drink. "I guess life just keeps moving on, whether we like it or not."

Joe understood perfectly. Not so long ago, his social media feed was a parade of adventures with friends, snapshots of their carefree moments between hospital shifts. Now his notifications were filled with wedding invitations and photos of his friends' new babies. He knew why he couldn't have those comforts in his own life, but the reality still left him feeling isolated and abandoned. He had once buried these feelings in relentless work and fellowship preparation, but here, standing in the community center beside Lily, he couldn't outrun the ache of loneliness that struck him with a piercing clarity.

Joe left Lily for a moment to fetch drinks for both of them, feeling parched from all the mingling. As he made his way back, the DJ transitioned from lively music to a slow, romantic song, dimming the lights to create a softer, more intimate, atmosphere.

He caught a glimpse of Lily's profile as he approached. She watched the dancing couples with a wistful sadness that tugged at his heart. But as soon as she noticed his return, her face brightened with her usual warm smile, masking the fleeting melancholy he had seen moments before.

So Lily was just like him. Presenting one

image to the world—the version of her the world wanted to see—so that no one would see the turmoil in her heart. He wished she didn't feel she had to do that for him. He wished she felt safe enough to show him all of her, even the parts the world didn't understand.

She accepted the drink with a smile, then leaned into his space to speak close to his ear. "I'm glad we came here, Joe. Thank you for bringing me. You didn't have to do that."

Joe's fingers brushed the warm, soft skin of her inner arm, tracing a gentle path from her elbow to her wrist. He watched as a range of emotions flickered across her face. She looked down, surprised by the tender touch, and then met his gaze as he took her hand in his.

"Care to dance?"

"Oh, Joe. You don't…"

"I know, I know. I don't have to be here." He slipped her hand into his and gently tugged her to the dance floor. "But have you ever considered that maybe I *want* to be here?"

Lily hesitated, her steps slowing as Joe gently pulled her toward the dance floor. "Here?" she asked, glancing at the gala's homemade decorations and the array of potluck dishes. "What would your friends in LA say if they saw you now?"

Joe looked down at the stunning woman beside him, feeling a surprising surge of emotion that only intensified at the thought of having her pressed close to him on the dance floor. But his feelings didn't matter right now. Tonight was about giving Lily a chance to create new memories in Twin Creeks, memories that would help her move forward when he was gone.

He gave her a playful grin. "I think they'd say Twin Creeks has grown on me."

She smiled at their shared joke and squeezed his hand. "All right, Joe," she said with a flirtatious shrug. "Let's dance."

Joe's shoulder had healed enough that he no longer needed to wear his sling, a freedom he now treasured for the way it allowed him to hold Lily close. He gently guided her hand to rest against his chest and let his free hand travel the length of her back until it found her enticing curves. As Lily melted into him, tucking her head under his chin, the scent of her shampoo filled his senses. He closed his eyes against the rush of emotions he felt. The sounds around them magnified. He could hear every note of the romantic song they were swaying to, and the low murmur of couples as they chatted, laughed, gossiped. Joe felt the warm and gentle press of Lily's body against his. He gazed at the delicate skin of her shoulder, longing to press his lips there and trace a tender path along the curve of her neck to her mouth. But that could never happen. Lily wasn't one of his casual just-for-fun flings that used to fill his days. And he could never promise her any sort of future that wouldn't break her heart if his family's cancer gene one day caught up to him. All he could have with Lily was this—the sweet torture of holding her in his arms, knowing she would never be his.

Lily pulled her head away from Joe's chest. "Joe?"

Joe opened his eyes, adjusting to the disorienting return to reality after being lost in Lily. "What?"

Lily stopped dancing and pulled away. "Something's wrong with Beth."

Joe and Lily hurried to Beth's side. She was bent over, her hands pressed to her swollen abdomen. Beth had visited the clinic for her prenatal checkup just before the dance. She was still a month away from her delivery date, but she hadn't been sure she should attend the event because she was feeling so many practice contractions. Lily had given her a thorough exam and encouraged her to attend.

But now, with Beth leaning against her husband for support, her eyes squeezed tight against the pain, Lily wasn't sure she had made the right call.

"Come on, let's get you some privacy," Lily said. She and Joe supported Beth as they walked her out of the gala event and to the classroom where they had held the blood drive. The Healthy Heart Association had not yet come to collect their borrowed equipment, so Beth was able to get comfortable in one of the recliners still there.

"It's okay," Beth said through gritted teeth. "This should pass in just a minute."

Lily thought back to Beth's last exam. Her readings on the fetal monitor had been low— much too low to indicate true labor. And her cervix was barely dilated. It was all consistent with a mother who was weeks from delivery.

Still, she opened her phone and noted the time. Just then, Beth gasped with pain.

Joe and Lily made eye contact. She could see unease in his eyes, too. This seemed too intense for practice contractions.

Lily gave Joe a little nod. A silent acknowledgment to keep things nice and calm until they knew what they were dealing with.

"Hey, Beth," Lily said. "Why don't we head over to the clinic? Let's get you back on the fetal monitor, see what's going on."

Beth held her husband's hand tightly. "But I'm not due for another month."

Lily tried to keep her laugh natural and light. "Well, you know. Sometimes babies have their own ideas."

Joe helped Beth get to her feet, then looped her arm around his neck. "Here we go, mom. Nice and easy."

But just when they got her back to her feet, Beth cried out and dropped to her knees.

"It's okay," Joe assured Beth, moving to support her weight.

"No, it's not!" Beth yelled, then started to cry. She wrapped her arms around her swollen midsection. "It hurts so much."

Lily knelt so she could look in Beth's eyes. "I think you're in labor, Beth."

That only made Beth cry harder. "But the hospital's two hours away."

Lily took charge. "Listen, Beth. I don't know if you're going to be having this baby in the hospital tonight. Joe has called emergency services, but I need to check you so we know what

to expect. If there's time, we'll get an air ambulance to take you to Billings."

"What if there's not?" her husband asked,
his voice tight with tension.

If they were lucky, Beth would make it to
the clinic where they had the equipment to
monitor mom and baby. Along with the labor
and delivery kit, medications and support for
the new baby.

"And if we're unlucky?"

Lily had to push the thought away. It was
time to think like a trauma nurse now. "We're
just going to take this one minute at a time,
okay?"

Joe sent a volunteer to the clinic with in-
structions on where to find their labor and delivery kit. Then he shouted orders for supplies
like soft blankets and a large lamp.

The sudden shift in energy made Beth even
more nervous. Lily took her hand and stroked
it gently. "Hey, Beth? You have just one job
here, okay? Keep your eyes on me. Everything's going to be okay. Let's keep taking
nice deep breaths now, all right? Let's give
that baby plenty of oxygen."

Lily snapped on a pair of latex gloves, then
checked Beth's cervix. She couldn't believe it.

Beth was fully dilated. Something round and hard pressed against her fingers.

Lily looked at Joe and tried to keep her voice calm. "She's ready."

Beth suddenly moaned. Lily felt Beth's abdominal muscles contract hard under her hand.

"This…baby's…coming!" Beth moaned through gritted teeth.

"Yep, she sure is," Lily said, using her nurse-in-charge voice. But inside she was feeling waves of panic start to swirl. Even in a hospital with all of its fancy technology, there was so much that could go wrong. It was terrifying to think of what could happen right here.

Part of her wanted to run. To escape this stuffy dance hall and Beth's pain and the fear of all that could go wrong.

Her gaze frantically swept the room, finally settling on Joe. He watched her with calm eyes. "We've got this," he said, and she wasn't sure if he was talking to Beth or to her.

But it calmed her. Because he was right. *They* had this. She would be okay because Joe was there.

In nurse mode, she gave Joe the update. "She's fully dilated, baby is crowning. Mom appears ready to push. Let's have a baby!"

Joe doused his hands and arms in sanitizer,

then pulled on the sterile gloves from the dance hall's kitchen. "All right, let's get this show on the road."

Lily timed the contractions while Joe guided Beth through pushing. He must have done a good job, because after just three contractions, a full head of dark, curly hair crowned.

"Almost there," Lily assured Beth.

With the next push, the newest resident of Twin Creeks made her debut.

Joe guided the baby into the world, cradling her tiny body in his hands. Lily watched his face as he worked to clear the baby's airway. But instead of relief or joy, she saw concern etch deep lines in his forehead.

Oh, no... she thought. There was no wail. The tiny newborn lay limp in his arms.

Beth looked up, her eyes full of questions and fear.

Lily's heart sank. This was her worst fear. Some babies had trouble making the change from getting their oxygen from the placenta to breathing on their own. As a trauma nurse, she had resuscitated a few babies, using an ambu bag to force air into the baby's new lungs and get breathing started.

But they didn't have anything like that here.

There was only one thing she could do for Beth's tiny baby.

"Hand me that dish towel," she demanded.

She took the baby in one arm and rubbed her body vigorously with the towel. Warming and stimulating the baby's body could trigger her to breathe on her own.

Chest and body, turn baby over, now the back.

"And the bulb syringe!"

She used it to clear the baby's airway again and again, then returned to rubbing the baby's body as hard as she dared.

Beth's eyes welled with tears. "Is my baby…"

"She's going to be fine," Lily said with fierce determination. There wasn't a bone in her body that didn't believe this baby would make it. She just needed a little more time.

Rub the chest and body…now the back. Clear the nose and mouth.

Joe said, his voice soft, "Lily…"

Lily shook her head hard. "No, Joe," she said, her tone fierce. Nothing bad was going to happen to this baby. Not tonight. Not on her watch.

She was just about to repeat the process when suddenly, a beautiful, perfectly pitched, tiny cry pierced the air.

* * *

Lily gently turned the baby over, watching in awe as her purple color transformed into a radiant pink. A wave of relief washed over her, leaving her feeling weak and unsteady as she realized Beth's baby was going to be okay. With a tender touch, Joe took the baby from her arms, quickly assessing her breathing and heart rate before handing her back to her elated parents.

Lily sank back onto her heels, her heart full as she observed the powerful scene before her. Though she hadn't delivered many babies in her career, the sight of Beth and her husband's astonished faces meeting their daughter was breathtaking. It stirred a flood of memories for Lily—her first meeting with Alexa, a poignant mix of joy and heartache. Joy for Alexa's safe arrival and the painful realization that she would never know her father.

Swiping at her eyes with her fingers, Lily forced herself to focus on the moment at hand. This was a time for celebration, not self-reflection. With a determined smile, she turned to the proud new parents. "Congratulations, Mom and Dad. What's your daughter's name?"

CHAPTER TEN

LILY STAYED WITH Beth and her family while Joe ensured Beth was stable and healthy. When the EMT crew finally arrived, she felt the tight grip of tension release. Joe took care of the patient handoff, giving her the chance to slip away to the quiet solitude of the deck overlooking the rose garden.

The cold air hit her immediately, and she wished she had grabbed her jacket. But the chill was also a welcome relief, bracing her emotions and offering a reset after the long, emotional day. Alone now, the adrenaline from delivering Beth's baby faded, leaving her feeling weak, drained and exposed. The emotions she had been holding back began to rise, impossible to ignore.

She heard the sliding glass door open behind her. "Lily?"

Her heart lifted slightly at the sound of Joe's voice. "Over here."

His footsteps echoed across the wooden deck, a faint creaking accompanying each step. She stood still, trying to steady herself, but then she felt the warmth of fabric as Joe draped his coat over her shoulders. His gesture, so tender and kind, was too much. She lowered her head, unable to stop the tears that overtook her.

"Lily! What on earth is wrong?"

Joe's voice was full of concern as he spun her gently to face him, trying to read her expression. But all she wanted was to disappear, to melt into the shadows. Instead, she moved closer, feeling his strong arms wrap around her, pulling her into a protective embrace.

"Lily, talk to me. What's wrong?"

For several minutes, she couldn't speak. All she could do was let the tears flow, and for once, it felt good not to be the strong one. To let someone else take care of her, just like Jennifer had told her all those years ago.

When the sobs finally subsided, she pulled away slightly, wiping her face and wishing for a tissue. Like magic, Joe produced a handkerchief from the pocket of the coat draped over her shoulders.

"What's wrong?" he asked again, his voice soft.

"Beth's baby came early!" she choked out.

"But she's okay," Joe reassured her.

"I know," Lily whispered.

"So why are you crying?"

"Joe…" She pulled away, dabbing her eyes with his hankie. She hoped she didn't have mascara streaked down her cheeks. "That baby wasn't supposed to be here for another month."

Joe laughed. "I know, Lily, but you're a nurse. You know life doesn't always go precisely as planned."

"Exactly."

His brow furrowed, searching for an answer to her inexplicable response. "I am so confused."

Lily led him by the hand to two deck chairs overlooking the garden. "Beth did everything right. She kept all of her prenatal appointments and took care of herself during her pregnancy, yet her baby still arrived early for no medical reason that would explain it. It just…happened."

"Right…"

"And Connor left for work like he always did. He made a thermos of coffee, kissed me goodbye and then he left like he had a thousand times before. But he never came home."

Joe's eyes were full of concern and protectiveness. He knew she was upset, but he didn't know why.

"For the past five years, I've tried to create a perfectly safe world for me and Alexa. A world where I can protect both of us from heartbreak and loss…because we don't *do* anything that might break our hearts.

"I call it our *bubble world*, and to be honest, I find it stifling as hell. But I have truly believed that I was doing the right thing for Alexa and me. I didn't want her to hurt like I had when I lost Connor, and I sure as hell didn't want to ever grieve the loss of my daughter.

"But tonight I'm just not sure I believe in that bubble anymore. Because there was nothing Beth or you or me could have done to stop her daughter from coming early. It was just…"

"Fate?" Joe offered.

"I guess you could call it that. It's just the way things were going to be."

Lily trailed off, exhausted by the long night and her emotional outburst. Joe seemed to understand that she needed some quiet. He just held her hand as she sat and thought about the past five years of her life. She had never questioned her desire to protect herself and Alexa from danger and pain. But she had also never questioned the toll that this battle had taken on her. The signs were everywhere. Her anxiety to let her daughter grow up and experience life. Giving up the work she loved because it was too painful to talk through her memories in therapy.

How much more was she willing to sacrifice for the illusion of peace and safety? She looked down at the hand that was holding hers. Joe was out here in the freezing cold without his coat because he didn't want her to be alone. He wasn't even supposed to be here. Had his life gone the way he planned, he'd be in Florida right now, and she might never have attended the gala again.

Joe's life plan never included Twin Creeks, yet here he was.

She'd never planned to love again. But she could if she wanted. Because he was here.

"Joe?"

"Yeah?"

"Take me home."

Half an hour later, Lily flung the front door of her cabin open so hard, it crashed against the wall.

She backed her way into the cabin, clutching fistfuls of Joe's shirt as she met the passion and intensity of Joe's kisses with her own desire.

She slapped her hand along the wall, searching for the light switch, but knocked a stack of library books off the hallway table. "Crap," she mumbled against Joe's lips.

"Don't worry about it," he answered, breathless against her mouth. "We don't need any light."

She kicked off her shoes and threw her purse on the floor, then led Joe up the stairs the same way she led him into the house. Joe steadied her backward ascent with his hands on her hips.

Eventually, they dead-ended at her closed bedroom door. She fumbled behind her, trying to wrench it open, but the handle wasn't budging and she was so distracted.

"Wait," Joe said against her mouth.

"Oh, my God, for what?"

Joe pulled away, obviously reluctant to break off the passion that had consumed them as soon as they got in his car. Driving home had been a spectacular form of sweet torture as she could only allow her hands to roam his body, nothing more.

Joe pulled away so he could meet her gaze directly.

"What are we doing here, Lily?"

Lily looked at the chest she had managed

to bare as she led him up the stairs. Her fingers traced the contours of his taut belly as she cocked her head and arched an eyebrow.

"No, I know what *this* is," he said, indicating their shared space with an impatient hand gesture. "I mean, what are *we* doing here?"

"Oh. Right."

She let her hands drop from his body and leaned her full weight against the door. Her breath was coming in ragged pants, and she could feel her heart thumping in her chest.

She pushed hair away from her forehead. "I don't see that there is a *we*, Joe. You're leaving in a few weeks."

"So this is it—just a casual fling between friends, then?"

Her heart squeezed with something that didn't feel good. Neither *friends* nor *fling* really described how she felt about Joe. But she wasn't going to dwell on that. Theirs was passion with an expiration date.

"Exactly. A friends-with-benefits setup."

Joe leaned into her so he could nuzzle her neck. Her hands automatically searched for and found his thick, wavy hair. "And when it's time for me to go to Florida?"

She closed her eyes against the image. She would be lying to him and herself if she said it wouldn't hurt when he left. But she would know it was coming. She could prepare.

"We'll celebrate with pie at the Snowy Owl."

"Seems fitting." He leaned in, ready to resume their passionate kiss, when she remembered something that was important to her. She pressed her hands to his chest, stopping his approach.

"One more thing... Alexa can never know."

"That might be tricky seeing as she lives here, too."

She shook her head to show she meant it. "We meet at your place. Or the clinic. Never here, unless Alexa is gone. Agreed?"

Joe nodded solemnly. "Agreed." He studied her face for a moment, as if he wanted to memorize the planes and curves of her. Then he traced her jawline with the back of his finger before bending to kiss her so tenderly, so slowly, that she thought surely she'd fall to pieces right there.

The frantic sexual energy that had propelled them to this moment was maturing into something tender and sweet. His mouth hovered inches from hers. Her chest rose and fell in tempo with his shallow breaths.

He leaned closer, until his breath stirred

her hair, tickling her cheek. "Are you going to open the door, Lily?"

"Oh. Right." She found the door handle, gripped it hard and felt the stability of the door fall away, leaving her weightless for a moment. She might have fallen if Joe hadn't stepped forward, his good arm finding her waist so he could pull her to him.

Her bed was unmade, and her pajamas were thrown over the overstuffed armchair, but she could not give a damn. All she wanted was to feel his skin against hers. Her hands helplessly tugged at his pants as he kicked the door shut behind them.

They stumbled across the floor toward her bed in a flurry of kisses and hungry hands. She strained to meet his kisses, her weight balanced on her tiptoes. She felt his fingers, light and teasing, as they followed the contours of her neck. Every nerve she possessed went on full alert.

"You are so damn beautiful," Joe said, his tone reverent.

She didn't know about that, but she knew his hands were making her skin sing as they trailed from her neck to her waist. His hands found the curves of her breasts, then wandered to her back, found her zipper, and slowly, inch by inch, tugged the zipper from her back to her bottom without ever breaking their kiss. The strapless dress slipped from her body to pool at her feet, leaving her standing naked save for her black lace panties and high heels.

Joe's gaze traveled the length of her body. "You are the hottest lettuce farmer I've ever seen," he said, and that made her chuckle. Until he palmed her bare breast with one hand, flicking his thumb over her nipple until both were tight and beaded. The flock of butterflies Joe had set loose with his flirting was becoming a manic swarm of bees, their incessant humming felt behind her navel and at the apex of her thighs.

"My turn," she whispered. She found the buttons of his shirt in the dark. She slipped each one through its buttonhole, then slipped his shirt from his shoulders. She smoothed her hands over his chest, followed the hard muscles of his forearms and biceps. The curves of his shoulder reminded her that he was injured, which meant she would have to take the lead.

She took him by the hand and guided him to the soft, overstuffed chair in front of the window where she liked to drink coffee and read. She pushed him into the chair, and he laughed at her bossiness. She laughed, too, but it was a husky, knowing laugh. Her power was coming back to her. For the first time in a long time, she knew what she wanted.

She followed him into the chair, tucking her knees against his hips. That made Joe's eyes go all smoky, and his hands found her hips, bringing her down so that the hot, damp vee between her legs pressed against his stiffness.

Her hands found his hair and burrowed into its wild waves. Joe arched forward to meet her mouth, his hands still bracing her hips. His mouth and tongue were demanding more now. She felt it, too. The need, so long denied, was building in her. She ground against his manhood, feeling fireworks of sensation in her core. *Damn, this was good*, but not nearly enough.

Her fingers trailed the skin above his belt buckle, making his muscles tense and shiver. His fingers were stroking her back, neck to bottom. It felt delicious and shivery. She unbuckled the belt and pulled it loose, then unsnapped his pants.

"We need a condom," she whispered. But then she remembered that she had some in her bathroom. A dusty memory tickled the edges of her mind as she rummaged under the sink, past boxes of tampons and bottles of hairspray and gel. Something that felt like a warning.

But she was tired of her mind always warning her to *be careful...be careful...be careful.* Beyond using protection, she wasn't going to be careful. She was choosing to be alive and accept all the risks that came with living the life she had been given.

Tucking the foil package between her teeth, she slipped off her panties, making Joe's gaze go hazy again. His obvious desire for her made her feel powerful and wanted.

"Get over here," he murmured. He lunged forward to pull her to him. She straddled his lap, then his mouth was on her breast and his fingers stroked her sex, stirring passions in her she thought she had put to rest long ago.

What a fool she had been. She hadn't put anything to rest. She had only buried this part of herself deep inside her soul where it had lain dormant. Joe was like a mage, finding all of her missing pieces and putting her back together.

She tore the foil packet open and rolled the condom on. Joe palmed her breast with one hand, her curves filling the palm of his other one. She watched Joe's lids go heavy and his eyes dreamy as she sank down on him. She

gasped at the sublime sensation of their joining, letting her head fall back with pleasure.

Joe thumbed her nipple as she rolled her hips
over him. Liquid heat rippled from his thumb
throughout her body, making her shiver with
pleasure.

"God, Lily, you feel so good."

Lily wanted to agree, to tell him how every
roll of her hips was making him hit that magic
spot that made her moan. Joe's breaths were
coming shallow and fast, his fingers digging
into her hips. She doubted he would hear a
word she said, if she even had the strength to
speak.

She could smell his clean sweat and hints
of his aftershave—woodsy and warm—and
it made her squeeze around him, loving him
deeper.

"Damn it, Lily. I…don't…please…" The
edge of lust in his tone was all it took to send
her orgasm rolling over her like a tsunami.
From deep in her core, pleasure rippled out-
ward, making her melt into Joe. He grabbed
her shoulders and yelped as his bliss peaked
into a series of shuddering rolls.

For many long minutes, they clung to each
other like survivors of something death defy-
ing. Lily curled into Joe's chest, inhaling his

scent. He was like a raft, ferrying her back to the safety of the shoreline with every gentle rise of his chest.

The buzzing bees that moved from her core to her brain, pestered her with demands to know *What does this mean?*

It didn't mean anything; that was what they had agreed. But she couldn't deny that all she wanted to do was bury under the covers with Joe and feel safe and loved for the first time in forever.

But that was not what Joe was offering, and she had to accept that.

CHAPTER ELEVEN

JOE WOKE IN the early-morning light, the soft glow streaming through lacy curtains. An unfamiliar clock ticked steadily beside him, and the faint sound of a crow—or maybe a woodpecker—filtered in from outside.

Slowly, he became aware of the warm body nestled against his. Eyes still closed, he traced the arm draped across his torso, then lightly stroked the leg that was wrapped over his hips. Her head rested on his shoulder, her breath deep and steady, almost to the point of snoring. Without thinking, he let his fingertips begin to glide along her arm, savoring the smoothness of her skin, still in disbelief that this moment was real.

Memories bubbled to the surface of Joe's sleepy mind. He recalled the way they danced, how stunning Lily had looked, the torturous drive home and finally, the moment they were alone. He remembered her passionate body beneath him as they lost themselves to each other in the quiet of the night. They'd agreed—this was casual, no strings attached, no expectations. The only rule: Alexa could never know.

Lily had understood and agreed without hesitation, and Joe was relieved they were on the same page. Though he knew he'd already fallen for her, he was determined to keep that to himself. As long as Lily wanted nothing more than a fling while he was in Twin Creeks, this could work. He'd deal with his tangled emotions later, when he was alone in Florida.

Joe let his hand wander along Lily's leg until it found the round curve of her backside. An incessant buzzing was ramping up behind his navel. He rolled over so he could curve around her, then let his hands explore the soft feminine curves of her body.

Lily softly mumbled. "Whatever you do, do not wake me up. Because this is the best dream I've ever had."

Joe smiled as he began nibbling the back of her neck. That made her shiver and laugh, then she turned toward him, loping her arm around his neck. He was just about to devour her mouth when they both heard a door slam downstairs.

Lily's body went stiff, then she sat straight up in bed. "Oh, no."

"Mommy! I'm home!"

Lily suddenly swore, then threw off the bed-sheets. He watched in a sort of fascinated confusion as she began flying around the room, first in one direction, then the other. She snatched her robe from its hook in the bath-room and lashed the knot tight and fast.

"Joe. You've got to get out of here!"

"What?"

But she wasn't paying any attention to him. She dashed around the room grabbing his pants, belt and shoes. "Get out of bed!"

She was obviously upset and he didn't want to make things worse. They could both hear Alexa calling for Lily. "Where are you, Mommy?"

"Lily, it's going to be okay. We'll just tell her…"

"No, Joe! Don't you understand? We're not even one day into our deal and we're about to get busted by my daughter! I do *not* want Alexa to know about this. You've got to go!"

"But how?"

Lily stopped and thought, her expression frantic. "You parked out back by the garage, so hopefully Alexa and Jennifer haven't seen your car yet. Get your stuff and hide in my closet. I'll go distract her and when the coast is clear, I'll come for you."

"Mommy?"

Alexa's voice was impossibly close.

Joe jumped out of bed naked, his arms full of his clothing, and made it into Lily's closet one split second before he heard Alexa say, "There you are, Mommy! I was calling for you. Did you hear me?"

Joe felt a rush of relief that he had managed to get out of sight before Alexa saw him. He stood frozen, afraid to even breathe, as he listened to the sounds of them descending the staircase. When he was sure they were downstairs, he began getting dressed in the dark. It wasn't easy and he hoped he hadn't put his shirt on inside out.

Long minutes passed as Joe waited for Lily's signal that it was safe for him to leave. He could hear them downstairs, but he couldn't make out their words. He heard the sounds of breakfast being prepared—the refrigerator door opening and closing, the rattle of silverware being laid out for breakfast, and Alexa's giggles. Then the grind of the blender and then the smell of bacon.

As Joe stood there in the dark, holding his

shoes so he could silently escape the house, the strangest feeling came over him. It was something he had never felt before—the desire to go downstairs and join them for breakfast. And the fact that Lily wanted him up here in her closet and not downstairs with her and Alexa left him grumpy and out of sorts.

But he deserved this—he knew that much was true. How many women had gotten the same lecture from him? Boundaries around his time, his attention and most certainly his affection. He had never really thought about what it felt like to have someone tell you that they can only love you "this much." That you aren't important enough to be their everything. He'd always thought that as long as he was honest and up-front about his limits, everyone was happy. But Lily had been honest with him, yet being left behind in her closet was not making him happy at all.

Why couldn't he just open this door and join them for breakfast? Because of that damn cancer gene. He knew his odds—they weren't good. If he had inherited the gene, there was a 60 percent chance he'd develop cancer before midlife.

But that meant he might have a 40 percent chance of being fine. And what if he hadn't inherited the gene at all? It was only on his mother's side of the family, so there was a not small chance that he didn't have any risk at all.

What if he took that test and discovered he was fine?

Joe heard the oven timer ding, then the smell of sweet hot rolls made his mouth water. If he didn't have that cancer gene, then things could be different. He could be downstairs with Lily and Alexa right now. Maybe he could be a mortgage-and-minivan kind of guy after all.

The closet door swung open violently, startling him out of his reverie.

"Joe, get out."

He blinked against the sudden light after being in Lily's dark closet for so long. He felt disoriented and confused and now Lily was hissing at him. "I've sent Alexa over to Jennifer's to borrow some eggs. You've got to get out of here now!"

She pushed his car keys into his hand, then grabbed his wrist and pulled him from the closet. Everything was happening so fast. All he could do was surrender to her urgent requests and follow her downstairs. Before he knew what was happening, she had shut the back door behind him and was headed back down the hallway. She turned back one last time and mouthed the word *go!* before she disappeared into the kitchen.

After a few seconds of getting his bearings, Joe turned to leave. It was a long trip back to town from her cabin in the woods and he had plenty of time to think.

Apparently, Lily hadn't exaggerated when she said she was up for a fling. A fling and nothing more because she had made it quite clear that she didn't want to risk any part of her "real life" being affected by their fling.

It was wrong for him to feel rejected—they had both agreed to the terms. Casual, fun, passionate and short-lived. He sighed and decided there was no need to get that cancer test done. Cancer or no cancer, his life worked better when he put work first.

It was the end of the day, and Lily had just finished with her last patient. She sat at her desk, reviewing patient files, stifling a yawn— exhaustion weighing heavy on her.

No surprise, really. For the past month, she and Joe had been meeting at his place almost every morning before work. Their clandestine affair continued, and she couldn't help but smile at the thought of the creative—and undeniably sexy—ways they made use of that hour. Occasionally, she'd manage to arrange for Alexa to spend the night at a friend's house, allowing her to slip over to Joe's, parking in the back to keep their rendezvous under wraps. Still, she wasn't entirely sure they'd gone unnoticed.

Joe exited his exam room with Maggie following close behind, assuring her that he'd send her test results to a cardiologist in Billings.

"You can call me tomorrow morning," Lily said, offering a reassuring smile. "I should have some news for you by then."

Maggie's eyes sparkled with mischief. "Should I call here? Or at Dr. Chambers's place?"

Lily kept her smile in place, playing dumb, but inside, her heart sank. There were signs all over town that people knew what she and Joe were up to. Just the other day, the mailman handed her Joe's mail to deliver, and Edna at the Shop-n-Go had been suspiciously inquiring about Lily's health every time Joe bought flowers. She should've known better than to think they could keep their affair a secret. After all, no one keeps secrets in a small town—that was what she always said.

But as long as Alexa didn't know, that was all that truly mattered.

After Maggie left, Lily and Joe settled in to review their cases for the day, including Maggie's. They talked over the results as Joe went through the list of tests he'd performed on Maggie: blood pressure, cholesterol, EKG and a few others.

"Anything conclusive?" Lily asked, hopeful.

"Not really," Joe replied, leaning back in his chair. "Her blood pressure, cholesterol and EKG all look like those of a very healthy young woman. The only thing she reports is feeling these heart flutters during her daily run."

"Any suggestions?" Lily inquired, her curiosity piqued.

"Maybe," Joe said thoughtfully. "We'll need to see what the cardiologist in Billings has to say. She might need to go there for a more comprehensive test."

Lily yawned, standing up to stretch. "It's getting late," she said, her voice trailing off. "I better get…"

Suddenly, her head started to spin, and the room grew dim. She wanted to call out that something was wrong, but the words wouldn't form. From a distance, she heard Joe shout her name before everything went black.

"Lily… Lily… *Lily!*"

Someone was shouting her name from the end of a long, dark tunnel. Lily struggled to open her eyes, her vision blurry. There was Joe, crouched over her, his penlight darting back and forth as he called her name with a firm, commanding tone. The edge of panic in his voice made her want to reassure him that everything was okay, but her mind felt too foggy to form the words.

"What happened?" she managed to croak, her throat parched. She tried to sit up with his help.

"You fainted," Joe explained, his concern evident.

"That's weird," Lily murmured, trying to piece together what had happened.

"But you seem to be okay. Your heart rate and blood pressure are normal, so I don't think it's anything serious. Have you eaten today?"

"Yeah, eggs and pancakes at your house. Remember?" Lily said, struggling to get her footing. Joe assisted her, staying close.

"Right," he said, hovering nearby as she steadied herself. "I think it was just a fainting spell, Lily. Has that ever happened to you before?"

"No, I'm not really the fainting type," Lily said, attempting to brush off Joe's concern. His intense focus made her feel a bit self-conscious. Once she felt steady on her feet, she made her way to the restroom, needing a few moments to freshen her makeup and regain her composure.

As she walked, a nagging memory surfaced. She turned back to Joe, hesitating before speaking. "Actually, there was one other time…when I was pregnant with Alexa."

The color drained from Joe's face, leaving him looking as if he might faint himself.

"Come on," Lily said, taking his hand and guiding him to the waiting room couch. He sank heavily into the cushions.

"Maybe it's not related," Lily reassured him. "Just because I fainted during my pregnancy with Alexa doesn't mean it's the same this time."

"Right," Joe replied, his voice sounding distant, his expression one of sheer, stunned horror.

"Besides, we used protection every time, so there's very little chance that—" Lily began, but then she remembered their first night together after the Healthy Heart Gala. As she rummaged through her bathroom cupboard, she had felt uneasy. At the time, she had brushed it off as her overcautious nature trying to shield her from getting hurt by Joe. But now she realized it wasn't just that. The condoms had been under her sink for years, never replaced because she had never needed them. That night with Joe, she hadn't been thinking about the expiration date or their integrity; she had simply been grateful they were there.

Joe stared out the window, his hands pressed together in a tense steeple. "You can't be pregnant, Lily. You just can't."

Her concern for Joe's reaction was giving way to a deeper, more painful, emotion.

"Would it really be so terrible if I was?"

She knew Joe had been eagerly counting the days until he could leave Twin Creeks and start his career as an oncologist. She understood his reasons were noble and good, but she had given up pretending that she didn't care. The truth was she had fallen for Joe in a way that left her disoriented and vulnerable. She had tried to savor every moment with him while maintaining the facade that their relationship was just a fling. But she had never imagined that he might see her as an obstacle to his plans.

Joe opened his mouth to respond, but Lily cut him off. "You know what? Let's just find out."

In a haze of shock and frustration, Lily stood up and headed to the clinic's medical supply cupboard. Joe's reaction had stung deeply, making her feel like a problem in his life rather than someone he cared about. Grabbing a pregnancy test, she made her way to the bathroom, hoping Joe wouldn't follow. Her emotions were on a knife's edge, and all it would take was a single word from him to send her spiraling into tears.

She peed on the stick and set it aside, waiting for the three minutes to pass. As she waited, she couldn't make sense of Joe's intense reaction. She hadn't planned on getting pregnant, and it was just as difficult for her as it was for him, but his horror seemed more profound than just shock. She knew how important his career was and that he was eager to return to his oncology training.

Despite her best efforts to keep their fling casual and free of commitment, she had fallen for him. She wasn't expecting him to change his plans because of a pregnancy, but it hurt to see that his shock seemed to go beyond the immediate news. He appeared truly horrified at the thought of her carrying his baby.

She glanced at her watch—three minutes had passed. Closing her eyes, she inhaled deeply, silently praying for the best. When she opened them again, she checked the results.

Joe was exactly where she had left him, slumped on the waiting room couch, his head buried in his hands. As she walked back in, he lifted his gaze to meet hers, his once-bright eyes now dull, filled with a hollow emptiness.

Without a word, she handed him the test. She watched as his breath caught in his throat, the color draining from his face.

Her heart broke. She sank onto the couch beside him, the weight of the moment pressing down on her chest. "Joe, I don't know what you think I expect, but... I don't have any illusions. I know you're not going to stay in Twin Creeks or...get married, or—"

Joe's hand gently curved over her knee, the warmth of his touch making her hate how her body instinctively responded to him.

"Lily, stop. This isn't about you."

"Then what is it?"

He sighed, hesitating, before finally speaking. "I should've told you a long time ago... but I didn't think it mattered."

Her heart thudded painfully in her chest. "What didn't matter?"

He took one of her hands, folding it gently between both of his. His voice was soft but heavy with grief. "My mom wasn't the only one in my family to die young from cancer. Her brother, father and my aunt—they all did, too."

"Oh, Joe...that's terrible."

"We didn't know it back then, but there's a gene. It runs in families. Different types of cancer, but the common thread—they all developed it before turning fifty."

Lily sat in silence, her mind racing as she pieced it all together. She couldn't even begin to imagine what it must feel like—so much loss in one family.

"We can test for that gene now," he whispered.

Shock rippled through her. "Joe, do you have the gene?"

"I don't know," he admitted, his voice low. "I've never been tested."

Her eyes widened in disbelief. "Why on earth not?"

"Because it didn't matter," he said, his frustration raw. "I had no plans to get married, no plans to have kids. I didn't want to risk passing it on."

Lily's mind flashed with memories of social media images—Joe at parties, on yachts, at the beach. Always with a beautiful woman, but never the same one twice. He hadn't been tested because he never planned to stay long enough for it to matter.

Not even with her.

A wave of emotions hit her—sympathy for Joe, who wasn't the player she'd thought, but a man hiding behind a mask of detachment. And fear—gut-wrenching fear. What if Joe did have that gene? He could have fewer than twenty years before facing the devastating diagnosis that haunted his family.

No wonder his oncology fellowship meant so much. It wasn't about ambition; it was his way of fighting the disease that had destroyed his family—and could one day destroy him, too.

But the fear didn't stop there. What if their child carried the gene? What if their baby had to watch Joe die young and face the same terrifying future?

"Joe, you have to…" Her voice broke, her chest tightening.

He raised a weary hand. "I've already called

a doctor friend of mine in Billings. As soon as I can get there, the test will be ready."

"I'm going with you."

"You don't have to—"

She grabbed his hand, gripping it tightly, her heart pounding with determination. She loved this man—desperately—and there was no way she was letting him face his worst fear alone. "This affects me, too."

Joe's gaze dropped to her belly, then back to her eyes, softening with understanding.

"Okay."

Lily fumbled through her purse, her hands shaking as she finally found her phone. She quickly arranged for Alexa to stay overnight with Jennifer, giving herself enough time for the two-hour drive to Billings. Everything felt surreal, like she was watching her life unravel from a distance.

At the hospital, the staff was expecting them. Joe was whisked away to the back, leaving Lily alone in the waiting room. The silence was unbearable, thick with dread.

Her mind raced, thoughts spiraling in every direction. What if Joe did have the gene? What would that mean for him? For their baby? The fear clawed at her insides, cold and unrelenting. She couldn't shake the thought of their child growing up without a father, just like Alexa had. But unlike Alexa, this baby would grow up knowing their father, only to suffer the pain of Joe being taken from them far too soon, just like the others in his family. The grief felt suffocating—grief for something that hadn't even happened yet but lingered like a dark cloud, casting shadows over every hopeful thought.

And what if the test came back positive? Could she handle watching Joe, this man she had fallen for so deeply, battle the same disease that had taken so many from him? Could she really survive the heartache of losing Joe like she had lost Connor? It was her very worst fear coming to life before her horrified eyes.

Maybe it would be easier to let him go to Florida. Let him run from Twin Creeks and from her. Let him slip back into his life, away from the constant reminder of what could be lost. She could return to her safe little bubble, where she controlled her world, and her heart wasn't at risk of being shattered.

When Joe finally returned, the nurse followed closely behind, telling them that his doctor friend had put a rush on the results. "We'll call you as soon as we have them."

The drive back to her house was painfully

quiet, both lost in their own thoughts. The tension between them was heavy, unsaid words hanging in the air like storm clouds. Once home, Lily numbly put on the kettle for tea, going through the motions while her mind felt paralyzed by all that had transpired.

Suddenly, Joe's phone rang, its shrill tone piercing the dark quiet of her house. They both froze, eyes locking, the weight of a thousand emotions passing between them. Fear. Hope. Love.

He answered the call, his hand trembling slightly. Lily reached for him, her fingers entwining with his. She wouldn't let him face this moment alone.

Joe listened in silence, nodding slowly as the voice on the other end of the line spoke. When he finally hung up, his eyes were wide, disbelief washing over him. "It's good news," he said, his voice thick with emotion. "The results are negative. I don't have the gene."

Lily's breath left her in a rush, her knees nearly giving out as the overwhelming relief washed over her. She felt like she could collapse, the weight she'd been carrying for hours suddenly lifted. Their baby was safe. Joe was safe.

For now, everything would be okay.

But the relief was short-lived. Lily knew they couldn't go back to what they were before the pregnancy test turned positive. This was supposed to be a fun fling—a few passionate weeks until Joe left. But now everything had changed. They both understood too much, had seen the risks they were taking, and there was no pretending otherwise.

A wave of exhaustion crashed over Lily, making her body feel heavy. All of a sudden, all she wanted was sleep. Joe looked at her, and for a moment, they were frozen—trapped in a mess of emotions and unspoken feelings, neither of them knowing what to say.

"Maybe I should go," Joe finally said, his voice quiet, almost hesitant.

It felt like a test. Should she ask him to stay? Would it make any difference?

"A lot's happened tonight," she said softly, her heart aching. "We probably need some time to process everything."

His eyes searched her face, trying to find something—anything—that would help him make sense of her emotions. But Lily didn't know what she was feeling herself, and she had no idea what he'd see.

"You're probably right," he murmured, the

sadness in his voice unmistakable. It felt like defeat.

"I'll see you at the clinic tomorrow," she replied, the words feeling hollow. When they kissed goodbye, it was a chaste, closed-mouth affair, the passion that had once burned between them now overshadowed by the uncertainty of their future.

Lily stood on her front porch, watching as Joe's taillights grew smaller, fading into the distance as he disappeared into the forest. A soft, distant sound—a rustle in the trees—pulled her from her thoughts, making her wonder what, indeed, the future would hold for them now.

CHAPTER TWELVE

LILY SMILED AS she checked Beth and her newborn, marveling at how the baby was thriving. Beth's husband beamed with pride, unable to contain his excitement. He was the picture of a proud father, doting on his wife and baby, bragging about their little one's first month of life.

Lily, exhausted from her long, emotional night with Joe, could barely keep her eyes open. But there was no way she'd miss this checkup. Being part of moments like these, caring for families and watching them grow— it was what she loved most about her job.

After walking Beth and her family to the waiting room, she noticed Joe emerging from his exam room at the same time. It was clear he hadn't slept much, either. They exchanged a brief glance as he wished his patient well.

"Lily, do you have a moment?" Joe asked, his tone serious.

She nodded, said goodbye to the family and followed him into his office, her stomach twisting with anticipation. She'd been thinking about him all night, wondering what the test results meant for their future. But now, seeing the look on his face, she wasn't sure she wanted to know.

Joe closed the door behind them and turned to her. "I have some news."

Her heart raced. What could possibly top the bombshell of last night?

"The oncology program in Florida had a candidate drop out. They've offered me the spot—if I can start a month early."

Lily quickly did the math. A month early meant...now.

"I have to leave immediately."

Her mind scrambled to process the words, and she sank into the chair opposite his desk. Just hours ago, she had been trying to figure out what Joe's test results meant for their future. Now it seemed like there was no future at all.

"Well, that's great news," she forced herself to say, her voice hollow. "I'm really happy for you."

"Thanks." But there was no joy in his eyes,

just exhaustion and something else—something that looked like guilt.

"I was thinking…maybe you and Alexa could come with me," Joe said, his voice tentative.

"Oh?" Her head spun as she tried to reconcile his offer with the defeated look in his eyes. She cared for him deeply. Maybe more than she had realized until now. But this—this didn't feel right. Some secret part of her had hoped their fling might become something real, something lasting.

But his eyes told a different story. He looked strained, burdened. "I don't want to leave you here all alone," he added, the weight of his words heavy in the air.

That was when it hit her. Joe didn't want to leave Twin Creeks. But he wanted Florida more. And now, she and Alexa—and their baby—were complications.

"Take the fellowship, Joe. You deserve it."

"What about the baby?" His words struck her like a dagger. No mention of love. No confession of feelings. Just the obligation of a child.

Lily thought of Beth's husband, how he doted on his wife and their baby. That was what it looked like when a man chose you—

when he wanted to be a father and partner above all else.

Her heart clenched, but she held steady. *You knew what this was* she reminded herself. They had never promised each other anything beyond a few weeks of good sex and fun. She had been the fool to fall for him, especially when his carefree social media feed had shown her exactly what would happen: good times, good sex then goodbye.

And that was okay. She didn't need Joe. She loved him—God, she loved him—but she didn't need him. And she wasn't about to love someone who didn't truly love her back. Beth's husband had shown her what real commitment looked like, and that was what she and Alexa—and her baby—deserved. Nothing less.

"You can see the baby anytime you want, Joe. Just let me know when."

Joe blinked, clearly shocked. He hadn't expected this. It felt like a breakup, but with so much more at stake.

He opened his mouth, as if to protest, but then stopped, thinking better of it. "And the clinic?"

"I think I can manage until the new doctor is hired."

He gave her a long, appraising look, as if waiting for her to change her mind. But Lily didn't waver.

"I have no doubt," he finally said, though his voice was soft, defeated. His shoulders slumped as he let out a breath. "Okay, then. I guess I'll go pack."

Lily merely nodded, her heart breaking as she watched him gather his briefcase and personal belongings, shutting down his computer with an eerie finality.

"I'm sorry, Lily," Joe said quietly, his voice full of regret.

For what? For getting her pregnant? For leaving early? She couldn't be sure. Other than the pregnancy, everything seemed to be perfectly on schedule for him.

"I know," she replied softly.

He gave her one last searching look, but she held firm, refusing to let her emotions betray her. Moments later, the clinic door closed quietly behind him, and he was gone.

Joe leaned back in his chair, rubbing his eyes as he glanced at the clock on the wall. It was nearing the end of his shift, but his mind was still racing with thoughts of his patients. The oncology ward was always busy, filled with the quiet hum of machines and the soft murmur of conversations. He took a deep breath, refocusing on his computer screen to update his notes before his next patient.

His cell phone alerted, signaling another hospital task at hand. Joe stood up, smoothing down his white coat, and made his way to Room 214. He stopped by the nurses' station first for an update on his new patient.

"Hey, I just got a page regarding..." He checked his phone. "Mr. Roger Allen in Room 214. What's the story?"

The nurse paused her typing on the computer to roll her eyes. "Mr. Allen's here for evaluation and treatment of advanced colon cancer. The attending put orders in for a full battery of tests, which the patient has completed. But he's refusing a colonoscopy because—and this is a quote—*I know my wife says I have my head up my butt, but I don't think she meant that literally.*"

Joe chuckled. "Well, at least he has a sense of humor, right?"

"Yes, but Dr. Atkinson is losing his cool. Mr. Allen's treatment plan can't be finalized until he's completed all the testing."

Joe rapped his knuckles against the counter. "Right. Let me see what I can do."

Joe knocked on the door, then entered Mr. Allen's room. He found a middle-aged man staring out the window, his shoulders slumped and eyes distant. The man's pallor and gaunt frame were stark reminders of the battle he was facing. Joe approached with a warm smile, hoping to ease the tension in the room.

"Good afternoon, Mr. Allen. I'm Dr. Joe Chambers. How are you feeling today?"

Mr. Allen turned slowly, his expression wary. "Not too great, Doc."

"I can imagine," Joe said. "I think we can get you feeling better soon, Mr. Allen. But we need to complete all your testing first."

The man groaned and turned away from Joe. "This will be my fourth colonoscopy, you know."

Joe winced. Not a fun procedure for sure. "I'm sorry about that, Mr. Allen. Can I answer any questions to make this easier for you?"

"Yeah," he said softly. "When can I go home?"

Joe's phone went off again, alerting him that his department meeting would start in five minutes. The next ninety minutes of his life would be about budgets, protocols and research updates.

It was tempting to give Mr. Allen a quick

pep talk, then rush off for his meeting and hope for the best. No one would blame him. His entire team spent their time bouncing around patient care, administrative meetings and endless hours spent documenting every single thing they did. He had learned a lot about bureaucracy since joining the oncology team here, but patient care seemed to get lost in the shuffle.

Joe checked his watch. He really didn't want to spend the next two hours in a stuffy meeting listening to administrators tussle over budgets.

"May I?" Joe asked, indicating the chair next to the bed. Mr. Allen nodded. Joe slipped his lab coat off and folded it over the back of the chair. He removed his tie and unbuttoned his shirt a bit. Not the same casual attire he wore in Twin Creeks, but maybe it would help. "Where is home, Mr. Allen?"

"A little town called Pine Hill. Not much there, but it's home."

Joe's heart ached at the familiarity of the story. "I know a little about small towns, too. I spent six months in Twin Creeks, Montana. It's tough being away from the people and places you know, especially during times like these."

His mind's eye formed a perfect image of Lily as she lay sleeping serenely in bed with him. Her jet-black hair fanning across her pillow, her lush full lips slightly parted in sleep.

He couldn't believe how just the thought of her was enough to make his throat go tight and his vision get misty. It had been six weeks since he had left Twin Creeks. He thought that his busy schedule would ease his pain, but it was as fresh as if it had happened yesterday. Daisy seemed to feel the loss, too. He had found a five-star doggie daycare for her to attend while he was working, but she never seemed happy when he dropped her off. The director said she would adjust in time, but every day he found her by the gate, ignoring the other dogs and looking up at him with big, soulful eyes that seemed to say *take me home*.

He had heard hardly anything from Lily since he left Twin Creeks. She did send him some of Alexa's artwork, though, which he clung to like a lifeline, each colorful drawing a reminder of the family he'd left behind. He knew she was running the clinic alone and he had a million questions about how everyone was doing, but she never sent any messages—just Alexa's drawings. And he didn't know what to say.

He got the message loud and clear. *Stay away.*

Joe and Mr. Allen talked for a while longer. Joe enjoyed Mr. Allen's stories about his family and life back in Pine Hill. It reminded Joe of the people in Twin Creeks, and all they had taught him about caring for patients. He couldn't shake the feeling of guilt for leaving them behind.

Just as he was about to leave the room, Joe heard a sharp voice behind him. "Dr. Chambers, a word please."

Joe turned to see Dr. Martin, his program director, glaring at him from the doorway. He nodded to Mr. Allen and stepped out into the hallway.

"Yes?"

"You're spending too much time with patients," Dr. Martin snapped. "We have protocols to follow, and we need you to be efficient. You can't afford to be so…sentimental."

Joe felt a flash of frustration. He was sorely tempted to ask his program director if he knew this patient's name and what he was willing to fight for. But he doubted that would improve their relationship.

At the end of his shift, Joe sifted through his mail. There were the usual conference announcements and advertisements from pharmaceutical companies. He was about to dump the pile in his waste bin, when a thin, creamy envelope caught his attention.

He immediately recognized Lily's handwriting. He held the envelope for a moment before he lunged for his silver letter opener and made a clean slit across the top of the envelope. He expected this might be another of Alexa's drawings but no, it was something else. Black-and-white glossy photographs.

He slid them from the envelope, laid them out one by one on his desk. He turned on his lamp so he could see them better.

His eyes welled up as he realized what he was seeing. Ultrasound images of his unborn child, taken at Lily's twelve-week checkup. A small, quiet smile spread across his face as he traced the grainy pictures with his finger. Never had he felt such an overwhelming mix of wonder and love.

He checked the envelope again, hoping there might be a note from Lily. Something to let him know how she was doing, if she was okay...if she missed him. But there was nothing to relieve the aching loneliness that had haunted him every single day since he had left her behind in Twin Creeks.

And why should she relieve his misery? He had foolishly convinced himself that he would

be happier here in Florida, buried in a fellowship consumed by data and statistics, instead
of being with the woman who had taught him
what it truly meant to love. He deserved every
minute of loneliness here.

Joe stared at the images for a long time, his
heart aching with longing. He missed Alexa's
bright smile, her infectious laughter. And he
missed Lily's warm body, her sensuous kisses.
Six weeks had passed since he left. He should
feel more like himself by now. But he couldn't
shake the feeling that he had made the wrong
decision.

He was surrounded by a tropical paradise,
but he never went anywhere but work and
his apartment. He could say it was because
he was too busy, but the truth was, there was
no beauty in the world without Lily by his
side. The ocean without Lily was just a shark-
infested salty pool. A sunset dinner without
Lily was like eating cardboard. Who cared
about tropical breezes and sun-soaked days
when you woke up alone every morning?

How many more signs did fate have to send
him before he got the message? It was time for
him to care for *people*. His people! His beautiful, quirky, delightful people.

He opened his computer again and composed a new email.

I regret to inform you that I will be leaving the Oncology Fellowship Program at Florida State University, effective immediately...

A huge weight lifted from his shoulders, and he felt joy coursing through his body for the first time in six long weeks.

Then he opened a new window so he could search for the first flight back to western Montana.

CHAPTER THIRTEEN

THE TWIN CREEKS COMMUNITY CLINIC was eerily quiet, a stark contrast to the daytime bustle of patients and activity. The hum of the fluorescent lights seemed louder in the absence of voices and footsteps. Stacks of patient files cluttered Lily's desk, each one a testament to the endless stream of ailments and worries she'd managed throughout the day. She leaned back, feeling the weight of exhaustion press heavily on her shoulders.

Her eyes drifted to the chair across from her desk—Joe's chair. It had been six weeks since he left, but the memory of him sitting there, laughing and joking, was still vivid. She could almost hear his voice.

"And then he says…" Joe had barely been able to get the words out between chuckles. "That's not a lab sample. That's my lunch!"

Lily had lost count of how many times Joe had teased her into fits of laughter, her tears smudging her mascara as she begged him to stop. The clinic had felt so alive back then. She could still see his broad smile, lighting up the room as they shared yet another one of his medical school stories. Those moments had made the world seem brighter, more enchanting.

She shook off the memory, her smile fading into a deep, aching melancholy. Sighing, she stood to stretch her back and headed to the kitchenette, needing a distraction from the weight of the past.

Filling the kettle with water, she reached for a travel mug but paused. It was a memento from the Healthy Heart blood drive and gala. With a sigh, she pushed the mug aside and chose a plain one instead. *It's just a mug, Lily. Just a mug.* But that small act of denial tugged at her heart.

The tea brewed slowly, the steam curling upward, mirroring her tangled thoughts. She returned to her desk, opening the next patient file, but her gaze kept flicking to the empty chair across from her. Why was it even there? Other than the occasional visiting doctor or nurse, she worked alone.

"Stupid," she muttered. Frustrated, she pushed away from her desk, grabbed the chair and dragged it across the room, the legs screeching against the hardwood floor. She shoved it up against the wall. "There!" she said to the empty room.

But it wasn't enough. Joe wasn't coming back to sit in that chair with his mischievous grin and that perfectly tousled hair. No more end-of-the-day jokes or intense discussions about difficult cases. It was just her now, and the ever-growing pile of patient files.

The front doorbell tinkled.

Good grief, what now?

"We're closed," she called out, her voice tired and resigned. She waited, listening. After-hours drop-ins weren't common, and usually, they were quick questions or requests for medication refills. If it was urgent, they'd stay. If not, she'd hear the doorbell again as they left.

Please, just go away.

Her body ached, and all she wanted was to crawl into bed with a cup of tea, a good book and maybe a sleeve of chocolate cookies. But then she heard a soft jangle—metal on metal—and a rustling sound.

"What the—?"

Before she could finish, Daisy appeared around the corner. Her ears flopped, eyes bright, her tail wagging with each step. But what really caught Lily's attention was the pink gift bag clutched in Daisy's mouth, a silver heart embossed on the front, the white tissue paper rustling softly.

Lily stared, her mind struggling to make sense of what she was seeing. Daisy padded around the desk and sat in front of her, tail wagging, waiting patiently. There was a small tag attached to the gift bag.

Open me

Lily's heart skipped a beat as she reached out, her voice soft. "Daisy, give."

The dog released the bag, and Lily retrieved it, her emotions swirling. If Daisy was here, Joe couldn't be far behind. She had spent weeks wondering if he'd miraculously appear like he had that dark, snowy night. She hadn't just waited—she had *yearned* for him.

She opened the bag, finding a small white box wrapped in tissue paper. Her fingers trembled as she removed it. Inside was a titanium cuff bracelet, delicate snowflakes etched across its surface. She flipped it over, noticing an inscription on the inside.

Fate 46.1263° North and 112.9478° West

"It's beautiful," she whispered, sensing Joe standing in the doorway. "But what does it mean?"

"Those are the GPS coordinates the mayor gave me the night I got lost in the blizzard."

Lily rolled the bracelet between her fingers, its weight solid and grounding. "You really hurt me, Joe."

She heard his sharp intake of breath. "I know. I was a bona fide idiot."

When she finally looked at him, he was as beautiful as ever—those magnetic blue eyes and tousled auburn waves—but he also looked thinner, tired. He glanced at the chair she had just pushed against the wall, his expression questioning. She nodded, and he dragged it back to its usual spot in front of her desk, sitting with his arms folded.

Joe took a deep breath. "I didn't choose you or the baby when I left, and I regret it every day. My whole life I've been preparing to fight the disease that destroyed my family. I never thought I'd have love in my life because of that risk. But then I met you, and it changed everything."

Lily held the bracelet tightly, her heart beating faster.

"My mentor sent me to Twin Creeks to teach me to care about people, not just the diseases they carry. I didn't understand what she meant at first. But now I know—she wanted me to learn who *I* was willing to fight for. And that's you, Lily. You, Alexa and our baby."

Joe's voice cracked as he continued. "I don't deserve anything from you after leaving, but I want you to know that I'm staying right here in Twin Creeks. I want to be part of my child's life—and yours—if you'll have me."

Lily rolled the bracelet between her thumb and forefinger. "Fate can be awful sometimes. That's what I told you that night."

Joe smiled. "I remember."

Lily held up the bracelet so that the light from her desk lamp glinted off the snowflakes. "But now I know that it can be pretty wonderful, too." Unconsciously, her free hand found its way to the beginning of her soft round baby bump.

She set the bracelet on her desk. Joe visibly stiffened. "I can't go back to the bubble, Joe. I've tried. But nothing works...because I'm in love with you."

He seemed too restless to stay seated. Joe crossed the distance between them, kneeling in front of her, his hands resting on her knees. A rush of electricity surged through her, making her certain their baby felt it, too.

"Oh, Lily," he murmured, his voice filled with regret. "I'm such an idiot."

She smiled softly and reached out to run her fingers through his thick tousled hair. "Go on…"

Joe took her hand, intertwining their fingers. The warmth of his touch felt like being wrapped in her coziest blanket. "You once told me that people aren't just problems to be solved. I learned that here in Twin Creeks. And again in Florida. People are more than their diseases. They're families, friends…and with you, I realized, they're the people you're willing to fight for."

His gaze dropped to her baby bump, then back to her. With a nod, she gave him permission. He placed his hands gently on her belly, his touch reverent.

"And I want to be here with you and Alexa and our baby, if you'll let me."

Lily's heart clenched as she fought off the voice that told her she was safer alone. Safety was an illusion anyway. Every day was an unknown, and maybe Joe or she would someday become a cancer patient themselves. But love was worth the risk.

"It's good to have you home, Joe."

Relief washed over his face. He slipped the bracelet onto her wrist, his fingers lingering as they both took each other in.

"Is this real?" she whispered, her voice trembling. "Or am I dreaming?"

"You tell me," Joe replied, his voice thick with emotion. He cupped her face in his hands, and when his lips met hers, the world faded away. She opened herself to him, mind, body and soul, ready to fight for their love for the rest of her life.

EPILOGUE

THE WHIR OF the helicopter blades was deafening, but Lily was used to it. The confined space of the medical chopper was her domain, and here, every second counted.

The call had come in just twenty minutes ago—a severe car accident on a remote highway. Now she was midair, speeding toward the crash site, her mind already racing through protocols and procedures.

"Let's move, people!" Lily shouted when they landed. She grabbed her flight bag and rushed to the patient, her heart pounding with adrenaline.

"Vitals?" she asked, kneeling beside the young man.

"Blood pressure's dropping, pulse weak," a paramedic responded. Sweat beaded on his forehead.

"All right, we need to get him stabilized before we can transport." She turned to her partner, Jake, who was already setting up the IV. "Two liters of saline, wide-open."

Lily assessed the injuries with a practiced eye. The man had a deep laceration on his thigh, likely from a piece of metal, and his chest was rising unevenly—a sign of potential internal injuries. She noted the pallor of his skin and the rapid, shallow breaths.

"He's in hypovolemic shock," she muttered. "We need to stop this bleeding now. Hand me the tourniquet."

With no hesitation, she applied the tourniquet above the wound, tightening it just enough to slow the blood loss without causing further damage. The man's eyes fluttered, and he let out a weak groan.

"Stay with me," Lily said through gritted teeth. "What's your name?"

"P-Paul," he managed to whisper.

"Hey, Paul, listen up, all right? Everything's going to be okay, Paul. I will make sure of that."

Lily and Jake worked together without saying a word. They had partnered on many rescue calls, and Lily had come to trust that he knew the right thing to do at the right time.

Lily secured an oxygen mask over Paul's face and checked the monitors attached to him.

"Good job, team. Let's get him on the stretcher and into the chopper."

The transfer was smooth, Lily's team moving like a well-oiled machine. Once inside the helicopter, she secured Paul and rechecked his vitals. He was still critical, but stable enough for transport.

As they lifted off, Lily monitored him closely, her mind already running through the next steps. She mentally prepared the detailed report she would deliver to the trauma team waiting at the hospital.

"Hang in there, Paul. We're almost there."

The city's skyline appeared in the distance, then the hospital's helipad came into view. Lily's grip on Paul's hand tightened for a moment, a silent promise that she would see this through.

They touched down, and the trauma team swarmed in, taking over with practiced efficiency. Lily briefed them quickly, then stepped back, her job done for now. She watched as they wheeled Paul away, a mixture of exhaustion and satisfaction settling over her.

That was the last call of her shift with Jake. All that was left to do was let the medical helicopter take them back to the air ambulance headquarters where her gear was stored. She said goodbye to the pilot and to Jake, grabbed her gear and headed for the parking lot.

Joe's forest green SUV waited in the parking lot, as she knew it would be. Even though it meant traveling an hour each way from Twin Creeks, Joe insisted on picking her up at the end of her twenty-four-hour shifts. It was a good call. Sometimes she was so bone-weary from back-to-back trauma calls, she could barely keep her eyes open.

But this pickup was a little more special.

Joe stood outside his SUV for her, and her heart almost skipped a beat. He was wearing the same jacket that he had worn the first time they had met at the Shop-n-Go and had his beard trimmed to that same precise short length. There was such a strong sense of déjà-vu, it made her knees a little wobbly.

He looked the same, but everything was so different now.

Jacob, their son, was eight months old now—a cheerful babbling baby. Alexa was halfway through first grade and delighted in her new role as Jacob's big sister. Both were waiting in the back of Joe's new SUV for their next grand adventure.

Lily walked into Joe's waiting arms and buried her cold nose against his warm neck. He wrapped his arms around her and rested his chin on her head.

"How did Jacob sleep last night?" she asked, breathing in the mix of his aftershave and baby powder and that unique scent that was just Joe.

"Well, let's put it this way," he said, his voice gritty with fatigue. "Whoever coined the term *slept like a baby* has a pretty warped sense of humor."

She laughed and looked up at him. He kissed the tip of her very cold nose.

"You ready for this adventure?"

Lily's heart fluttered a little as she contemplated their family's first ever ski trip. It had been a long time since she had donned a pair of skis and hurled herself down a mountain, though she doubted that was how this adventure would go. With two kids under six, this trip would be less black diamond, more bunny hill for sure.

"I've been counting the hours," she told Joe, then handed him her flight bag. He headed to the back of the SUV to store her gear along with their suitcases and skis while she opened the back passenger door to find her two rug rats waiting.

"Mommy! Joe said we're going skiing!"

"That's right, baby. We're leaving right now."

Alexa's face furrowed into a small frown. "Will I get to go skiing, too?"

Lily's heart fluttered at the thought of Alexa on skis, but she pushed the fear aside. "Of course you can. But you have to wear your helmet and stick to the bunny slope…"

"Aww, Mom!" Alexa, her beautiful, stubborn, ambitious, adrenaline-junkie daughter protested.

"Until," Lily continued with a smile, "the ski instructor says you are ready for the intermediate ski runs."

Alexa's eyes widened at the prospect of more thrills ahead. "Okay!" she said with a beaming smile. She had something to look forward to now, and really, wasn't that what everyone wanted?

Lily leaned forward to give her dozing baby a kiss on his forehead. He still smelled like a baby, which was a source of endless delight. "No skiing for you, baby Jacob," Lily whispered. "You'll be having fun at the lodge's childcare center."

Alexa looked at Jacob like she was a little mother, too. "Don't worry, Jake. When you get bigger, I'll teach you how to ski."

Joe appeared behind her and wrapped his arms around her waist, tugging her into his chest. She took a moment to lean back into him, loving the solid feel of his body against hers.

"You ready for this?" he asked, his breath warm on her ear.

Lily paused for a moment to reflect on the adventure her life had become. After becoming a mother for the second time, she and Joe had worked together to design a new home for themselves, located a little closer to town so they were better able to respond to urgent calls at the clinic. Jennifer was sad to see them move away, but it also meant she could rent out her cabin to the many tourists who passed through Twin Creeks.

Joe and Lily ran the Twin Creeks Community Clinic together now. They had developed a business plan focused on adding new services and technology to better serve Twin Creeks and its surrounding communities. Joe volunteered one week each month with Trailblazers in Cancer Care, delivering cancer treatments and doing preventative screening in towns in the wider area.

Lily had started taking a few shifts each month as a flight nurse with an air ambulance company based in a small town about an hour outside Twin Creeks. Working in trauma care again, even on a limited basis, thrilled her and sharpened her skills for emergency work that came up at the clinic.

It also made her feel connected to Connor in a mystical way. Of course she saw Connor in Alexa, too, especially in her beautiful hazel eyes. But it was in the skies where she most felt Connor's presence. They had bonded over the high stakes trauma cases she had delivered to his emergency room, and every patient she stabilized and saved made her feel close to Connor, even if it was just for a moment.

She glanced up at the skies now, and then to Joe, who had helped her weave her past into her future.

"I sure am," she breathed. Then she turned and took Joe's coat lapels in her hands, so she could pull his mouth down to hers. His kisses were like oxygen to her, and she inhaled him deeply, feeling his love permeate her body so that every doubt was subdued, every lonely corner filled with warmth and hope.

* * * * *

*If you enjoyed this story,
check out this other great read
from Kate MacGuire*

Resisting the Off-Limits Pediatrician

Available now!

HARLEQUIN
Reader Service

Enjoyed your book?

Try the perfect subscription for Romance readers and get more great books like this delivered right to your door.

See why over 10+ million readers have tried Harlequin Reader Service.

Start with a Free Welcome Collection with free books and a gift—valued over $20.

Choose any series in print or ebook. See website for details and order today:

TryReaderService.com/subscriptions